KNOCKED UP BY MY BULLY

KRYSTAL CLARK

INTRODUCTION

This book contains explicit scenes between consenting adults. All characters and events are fictional. The author does not endorse the characters' beliefs or behavior.

The book contains material that may be offensive to some including: breeding kink, lactation kink, adult nursing, hucow, coarse language, instances of verbal racial stereotyping from the MC's dad, accidental pregnancy, pregnant sex, pregnancy kink, and a dominant bully with a filthy mouth. If you don't like any of that, don't read.

ONE

Saint

I'M SUFFOCATING on the smell of expensive perfume.

"Saint, oh my gosh, you're with Hannah King!" A girl whose name I don't know shrieks in my ear. She's looking at a photo of me on Instagram. It was taken last night. In it, my arms are around a leggy blonde actress who was too desperate for my attention.

I tap my fingers against the desk, waiting for the class to begin. I swear, I should be late to all my classes. All I get for being early is a herd of stupid girls with fake tits trying to seduce me. The only reason they're trying so hard is because of my last name.

I'm David Cross's eldest son, the heir to an empire worth billions of dollars. These chicks want the lifestyle that comes with that kind of money. Designer clothes, exclusive after-parties, rubbing shoulders with celebrities. They're vying for the position of the future Mrs. Cross.

Too bad I have no interest in offering it to them.

"Can you introduce me to her?" She puts her lips close to my ear. "I'll give you whatever you want in return."

My head throbs when she pushes her tits to my face. Her push-up bra and fake tan are trying to make her seem like something she's not.

To me, it's boredom. Same looks. Same glances. Same girls, different day. I turn my face toward the door, waiting for the one girl who is different.

Jennifer Garcia.

When Jennifer walks in, I hear her denim skirt swish from halfway across the room, a sound so honest it makes my teeth hurt.

Her tits rise from a scoop-neck T-shirt, and my fingers ache. Her brown eyes, that perfect tawny skin, it all has me obsessed, thinking crazy, desperate things. I want her legs over my shoulders. Her hair spilling across my chest. To know every secret. I want all of it. I want all of her.

I think she rolls her eyes when I move closer. A new perimeter forms around me. The girls fawning over me quickly rearrange themselves to crowd around me. I catch snatches of conversation. Parties, rumors. Maybe if they're lucky, someone else famous will come along, and they will lose interest in me.

Before I know it, a blonde in workout gear lands next to me, her lipstick brighter than her IQ. "You should totally follow me," she says, managing to make it both a demand and a plea. "Follow you where?" I ask, pulling her heart right out of her perfectly toned chest before she's even sat down.

Next comes a soft punch to my arm and a "You're bad," but not too far behind, she makes sure to include a hopeful, "But I love bad."

She scoots closer, latching on as if I'd planned to drift away, and that's when it happens. Jennifer takes her seat, acting like it's all coincidence, like she hasn't just sat within throwing distance of someone about to make her do things I haven't even made her imagine yet.

One last glance confirms she's the only one with the nerve. Or the stupidity. Or whatever it is that makes her so fucking different. Same crossed legs, same uncrossed. Like she's flaunting herself without meaning to, like every goddamn part of her isn't exactly how I need it to be.

Her supple tits, lush but definitely real, pop out of her scoop-neck T-shirt. Her hips are wider than the highway. In the past, people would call those baby-bearing hips. Her ass is huge and round, straining against her tight jeans. She's beautifully shaped, like a feminine goddess. Her lightly tanned skin, curly dark hair, and hazelnut eyes give her an earthy sensuality. Raw, real, powerful, seductive. There's something primal and feminine about her, something that calls out to me.

Her dark gaze sweeps over me briefly before she pulls it away.

And then, the knife to my guts: she ignores me.

Instead, she tugs a book from her bag, gives it the attention that's mine, should be mine. The fucking economics textbook, perfect in its hardcover arrogance, staring back with glossy, reproachful looks, rubbing in how lucky it is, how lucky I'm not.

The professor clears his throat. The lecture starts, something about macroeconomic policies, but none of it has anything on Jennifer. Her scoop-neck rises and falls with this quiet persistence that I don't understand. How she's so different, how she can stay that way. Not a hint of makeup on her, not even a touch of product in her curly hair. She's earth and fire, and the whole world bends around her, including me.

Not that I don't get other options. I could drown in them. They're everywhere, like that couch I almost ruined with a gorgeous sophomore just last week, and I didn't even catch her name. Jennifer's phone buzzes and her attention moves from her book to her phone. That's not usual for her. Her plump lips press into a line. I can tell whatever she read on her phone isn't good news.

I watch her and imagine how I'll get what I want. How I'll push and push and get under her skin like she gets under mine. I don't do patience, but for her, I've been trying. Been watching the signs.

Three months ago, she told me "Get lost" with her cold gaze.

Three months ago, I took it as "Try harder."

Some girls still hope for a glimpse of Cross gold, wait in agony for that single glint to bless them. I'm the son of a billionaire. I'll take over my dad's multi-million-dollar company in the future, whether or not I graduate with a degree. Any girl who marries me will live a life of luxury. She'll never have to lift a finger.

But none of that matters to Jennifer Garcia. All she cares about are her grades.

That's why I'm obsessed with her. She's not a gold digger. She's not even remotely interested in me. And my ego is bruised at the thought of being less interesting than her textbook.

"Pay attention, this will be on next week's test," the professor says.

The lecture drones. I make sure to look interested, jot down a few meaningless phrases so that anyone watching thinks I actually care about this degree. I don't. I care about my stepbrother, the one person worth a damn in my life. The list ends there.

The long-ass lecture finally comes to a close. I see her close the book.

I swing my bag over my shoulder.

But instead of leaving, I creep closer to her. I'm not going to do anything stupid. I just need something from her.

Jennifer's buried in her phone. And now I see why: there's a picture of her on the screen. A nude pic. Her tits are out on display, capped with perfect brown nipples. Her hourglass figure is spread on a white bedsheet, with a comforter draped over her pussy to hide it from view.

My cock stirs. Heat flows through me like a volcano about to erupt. Damn, she looks even hotter naked than I could have imagined.

I need to get my hands on her body, even if I have to black-mail her. I pluck out my phone.

She doesn't notice at first. How close I am. How my phone is ready. But when she does, it's like catching a fish with your bare hands. She doesn't think it will happen, not to her, not to the perfect Jennifer Garcia.

She's all mine for at least a few seconds, caught off-guard, a faint crack in her always-know-the-plan expression.

The picture of her naked flashes on my phone. It's stored in my gallery. I just clicked it when she let her guard down.

That's my ammo.

Jennifer gasps when my camera goes off again.

She turns back, shocked when he sees me. "What did you do?"

"You were looking at something interesting so I thought I'd take a picture, too."

"No." Her voice drops. "That's not meant for your eyes, Saint. Delete it."

She claws at my T-shirt but I'm 6'3 and she's 5'2, so there's no way she can reach my phone.

"Careful. My dad will sue you for millions if you scratch me."

I expect her to ignore my warning but she must be pressed for money. She stops flailing her arms. I keep a tight hold on my phone. After months of having her slip through my fingers, I have something interesting on her. I'm going to use it to get close to her. I need to figure out why I'm fascinated by her, why she lives rent-free in my head even though I forget the girls I've fucked within minutes.

"You're a total prick," she says. I like how her mouth wraps around it. How it fits.

"That's the rumor," I say. "But you'll have to get to know me first."

She snaps the phone case shut, keeps her arm around it like I'll wrestle it from her perfect, protective fingers. I glance down. The fabric of her scoop-neck clings like a second skin. I clench my fist, stop myself from reaching out to feel it.

"You didn't seem like the type who wanted the chase," she adds.

"I didn't before I met you."

I hold up the phone again, showing her incriminating evidence. Jennifer sighs. "'You really managed to take a pic. You should switch majors to photography. Your real talent isn't in the business field."

I steal her phone from her.

She gasps. "What do you want?'

"I'm deleting the photo. Pro tip, Ms. Garcia: delete your naked selfies before anyone else sees them. Especially the ones that show your hard nipples in high-definition." Her eyes widen like I've just flashed her a rare gem. "Maybe you forgot I can zoom."

She groans in frustration as I throw her phone back to her. She catches it.

"You boyfriend doesn't deserve to see you like that." Jealousy pricks me.

"I don't have a boyfriend," Jennifer snaps. "Girls can take sexy photos of themselves just to feel good. It's not always for a guy."

I rub my chin, impressed. How does she manage to make me admire her every time I talk to her? "You have more self-respect that I gave you credit for."

"Please delete the one you have." She crosses her arms, pushing up those perfect tits over her scooped neckline. The glimpse of her plump, perfectly shaped boobs makes my groin cramp with need. Now I know how they look bare, the desire to suck on her hard nipples is a wildfire tearing through my system.

I drag my fingers through my silky hair. "I will. On one condition. You have to babysit my brother."

She gives me that look again, the wide-eyed, dazed-for-a-second look. It's even better the second time around. I could watch it unfold forever. Maybe I should grab her and stop it with my tongue in her mouth, my fingers digging into her ass, leaving marks that she'll trace with disbelief.

"Wow," she says. Her tone is bright. "Creative."

"Clever too," I say. "Not just another pretty face."

"I'm a crappy babysitter," she says, sharp and loud and perfect. "Haven't done that since I was, oh, thirteen. I have no clue what you think you're doing."

"Don't care."

She rolls her eyes. "By the way, I didn't know you had a brother."

"He's about to turn two. I have better things to do so I need you to watch him in the evening and put him to sleep. I'll pay you twenty-five dollars an hour."

"And you'll delete the photos." It's a statement, not a question. I mistook Jennifer for a shy, nerdy girl because she doesn't talk much in class but she's a spitfire. She keeps her strong personality hidden underneath her quiet exterior. I'm more and more intrigued.

"Sure." I roll my shoulders, tapping on my phone. "I'll see you at my place at six. Give me your number."

Her defenses come back up and she pulls back, physically widening the distance between us. "Why?"

"I need to text you my address."

"Oh." She stammers. "Right."

I get her number, don't waste a second, lock it down with the street and apartment.

"He's a cute kid," I add. "Like I said, I'll even throw in $25 an hour for your services."

"I guess money does grow on trees for some people." She picks up her bag, slides it across her shoulder.

She moves for the door, casual, so goddamn sure of herself. But not enough to forget what I'm offering. It's her strength. It's her weakness. I can't wait to find out. I can't wait to find out all of her. She's different, a puzzle I can't figure out.

That's why I keep watching.

With all the right conditions, who knows what might happen? After all, even saints fall.

TWO

Jennifer

I CAME HERE for the money. Twenty-five an hour isn't anything to joke about. That's way more than I'd make at my part-time job.

Saint lives in a townhouse off-campus. I live with my mom, so I also live off-campus. However, our neighborhoods couldn't be more different. They're on opposite sides of town, separated by an invisible economic barrier. While I live in a middle-class suburban hell, Saint inhabits the most exclusive postcode. The brownstones here cost millions of dollars. The streets are quiet, wide, and lined with trees. Pink flowers are in full bloom.

I snap a picture of the area with my phone. It's so photogenic, like something out of a postcard. And this isn't even his actual house. He's renting it. His parents live in Boston, while we go to school in Fall Creek, a town that's three hours away.

I end the navigation on my phone as I arrive at a pretty townhouse. I climb up five steps to reach the entrance.

The door alone is jaw-dropping. There are iron griddles on it, as well as two Victorian lamps on either side. If that wasn't grand enough, there's even a lion-shaped door knocker.

I don't know whether Saint lives alone or with roommates. But given his tyrannical temper, I doubt anybody would stick it out with him.

I snarl when the door opens and I'm greeted by the most perfect face God has ever crafted. I can't understand why the Almighty decided to waste his talents on Saint Cross but if there's one thing the guy doesn't lack, it's luck. He was born rich, handsome, smart, and with a sense of humor that should be illegal. The heavens bestowed him with every gift possible.

"You better pay me what you promised," I mutter.

"Come in and erase that scowl. You'll scare my baby brother." Saint steps back, letting me enter. I brush past his body. The hair rises on my body. My chest tingles. I've never been so close to him. He smells of fresh shower gel and privilege.

I have a hard time swallowing. His shoulders are broad and muscular. His biceps strain against his gray T-shirt. He's oozing sex appeal and raw masculinity. I have seen a lot of good-looking guys but Saint is in a league of his own. His attractiveness is visceral; I feel hotter just by standing next to him. It's no surprise all the girls are obsessed with him.

Saint hovers close to me, towering over me with his ungodly height as we cross the foyer, emerging in a neatly appointed living room. Even the air in his house smells like money. They must be spraying some luxury air freshener around here. I feel like I'm in a different world. A world of sophistication and things beyond my means.

"That's my brother." Saint points to a little boy with blonde hair who is watching TV. "Easton. He looks cute but he'll drain your energy in no time."

I'm not intimidated. Also, I don't back down once I've

committed to something. Despite Saint's menacing presence, his home is very comforting. Definitely better than mine. The thought of spending time in a nice environment warms my heart.

Plus, the money is good.

I have a scholarship but it doesn't cover my entire tuition fee. I still have to pay a portion of it. My mom barely makes enough to help me with it, though. I work part-time to avoid taking out a student loan. I don't intend to start my adult life with a mountain of debt.

"Feel free to grab yourself a drink from the kitchen before you get started." Saint turns his head right, where I can see the polished quartz countertops of his kitchen.

I can't resist the offer. I'd love to know what rich people drink, and what kind of stuff they have in their refrigerator. Saint slinks away, landing beside his brother. I'm surprised he left me on my own. He must trust me.

I notice how he ruffles his brother's hair and makes the child laugh. My chest tightens. I need to be careful. I don't know much about Saint Cross beyond what I've heard whispered around college. He's rich, smart, goes through women like underwear, and he's dangerous.

I refuse to get tangled up with him when I'm so close to graduating. Yet, seeing him make funny faces for his brother, I wonder if the rumors are actually true.

I close my eyes, blotting out the image of my bully. Saint consumes more of my thoughts than he should.

I march to the kitchen. The stuff in the fridge is fresh and well-organized but it's mostly food, apart from a six-pack of Corona. I guess rich people aren't so different after all. Why doesn't Saint's taste in alcohol surprise me? There's something grounded and earthy about him despite his exalted lineage, something that makes him approachable.

Since I'm not in the mood for alcohol and I have too much work ethic to be drinking on the job, I reach for what looks like green juice. I enjoy smoothies and juices every now and then, but I can't afford them every day.

I grab a glass and pour some into it. Then I sip on it slowly. The juice is sweet rather than bitter. It goes down my throat nicely, erasing the parched feeling in my mouth. I end up gulping down another glass. My stomach bulges as all that liquid gets in it.

I head to the living room. Saint is entertaining his brother, who has stopped watching TV now.

"Do you want to play outside?" I ask Saint's brother. "Fresh air is good for kids."

Plus, exercise will make him tired and I'll be able to put him to sleep easily.

"She's your babysitter," Saint explains. "Her name's Jennifer."

His brother watches me through wide blue eyes, staring at me like I'm a monster that came out of his worst nightmare.

"It's okay; I'll be keeping an eye on her. Why don't you go play catch?" Saint nudges his brother toward me.

Easton hesitates, but he comes closer.

"I'm a nice person. I just want to play with you." I caress his hair, giving him head scratches as he leans closer to me, resting his small head against my breasts. I rub his cheek, assuring him he's safe with me.

Saint leaves me to scurry up the stairs. When he returns, he drops a stuffed toy ball on my lap. I take it as a cue.

"The backyard's through that door." Saint cranes his neck, pointing his nose toward a stained-glass door that leads out of the living room. It's located on the opposite side of the door I entered through.

I gently guide Easton through the door, ball clutched in the other hand. The backyard is huge and the grass is well-kept. I throw the ball at Easton. He giggles as he lunges for it, grabbing onto it.

"Well done!" I clap.

We play for a while until it gets dark.

Then we return to the house where Saint hands me a bowl of mashed-up food. "Feed him. That's his dinner."

I help Easton clean up and change into his pajamas. He's used to me now so he is chattier. He doesn't know many words, but he talks about his trucks and how much he loves them. I realize I don't mind spending time with Saint's brother. For one, he's less scary and more innocent than his older sibling. I don't feel the hair rising at the back of my neck of goosebumps when I'm around him.

I especially don't feel the strange pulse between my legs.

But that heat returns when we exit the bathroom and join Saint on the couch. His presence clings to me like a curse. The point between my thighs grows warmer like someone's touching it.

I hate to admit that Saint has a sexual effect on me but it'd be more surprising if he didn't. He's hot as sin.

I feed Easton slowly while we watch a kid's show.

"So how did you end up babysitting him?" I ask Saint, hoping to clear the heavy tension in the air with a lighthearted conversation.

"My stepmom is sleeping with the dean." Saint yawns like he didn't just drop a bomb. I cannot fathom how he can act so casually about his stepmom's infidelity. Then again, I suppose that behavior is common among rich people. He must be used to it. "She comes over every week to have sex and makes me babysit her kid."

"Does your dad know?"

"Probably." He turns his head, searing me with a brutally

honest look. There's a hint of sadness in his eyes. He looks like a lost soul, trudging through a cold world that doesn't care for anyone, even people with money. "She doesn't cover her tracks well. But she thinks my dad is oblivious. I use her fear of being discovered to my advantage. I have a lot of shares in the company thanks to her foolishness."

I scoff. "So you're bullying her, too."

"I'm looking out for my little bro." He points to his younger brother, who is sucking on his thumb, unaware of the complex adult conversation around him. His glassy blue eyes, a mirror of Saint's, are fixed on his big brother as if he can recognize Saint. "If his mom decides to run away with another man or ends up getting a divorce, who'll protect him? My dad doesn't have the time to raise him."

"So you babysit him because you care about him?" I sound incredulous.

Saint sighs. "Who knows?" He pauses, scratching his jaw. It was clean-shaved earlier but there's a stubble dotting it now. It adds maturity and allure to Saint's already drop-dead-gorgeous face. This guy was born with an insane face card. The longer I spend in his presence, the greater my desire to lick his sharp jawline and perfect features grows. I curl my fingers into fists, forcing my horny thoughts to calm down. The last thing I need is sex with my bully.

"I was an only child," Saint continues. "It gets lonely sometimes."

I get it. He doesn't want his little brother to grow up alone in a household where nobody cares about him. I doubt his dad spent time with him when he was young. Saint doesn't look like the kind of guy with a happy childhood. You can see the neglect written all over his face. There's an air of strength to him, a cold disinterest common among people who have only seen transactional relationships.

He's more complex than I imagined. I wrote him off as a bully but there's more to him than entitlement and godly beauty. My heart pounds. I want to unravel him. My brain is interested in solving the mystery of Saint Cross.

"I'm an only child, too," I say. I'm not sure why I'm giving him more ammunition when he already has those nudes. Something about his aura makes me feel safe to tell him about me. He's rich but he doesn't seem judgmental. "My parents divorced when I was young."

He narrows his eyes. "Are you trying to get my sympathy?"

There's a cutting tone to his question, like he's wondering if I'm trying to take advantage of him, trying to get close to him like everyone else at school. I always thought being rich was a fantasy but maybe it's not all it's made out to be. I doubt Saint has had any genuine relationships in his life. The girls in college only want him because of his status.

"You know what? Forget I ever said that." I rock the child in my arms. Saint's brother is falling asleep. I was worried I'd struggle putting him to bed but he seems like the perfect child. "I'm going to take him to bed now."

"He sleeps with me upstairs," Saint calls to me. "First door."

He doesn't follow me. I appreciate the alone time. Being around him feels like choking on smoke. I can't escape his presence. It's larger than life, enveloping me, always reminding me that I'm inches from a literal god. He exudes magnetism and charisma, even when he's watching TV. I have never come across someone so...consuming.

I push the door open.

Saint's room is huge and quiet. There aren't any personal items, not even posters of sports players. The walls are sterile, hung with modern art similar to the paintings downstairs. It's like the entire house was decorated by an interior designer to resemble a rich person's house.

The bed is king-sized. Figures. Given the size of Saint's ego, he wouldn't settle for a single bed.

There's a crib beside the bed. My heartstrings tug at the idea of Saint sleeping with his brother, waking up at night to soothe him when he cries. There's baby food and a feeding bottle on his nightstand.

This looks like the room of a new dad, not a wicked heartbreaker. Saint might be a player but he has what it takes to be a responsible father.

I lay his brother in a crib. His small fingers lock around one of mine but I ease myself away. I wait for a few minutes to make sure he's fully asleep before sneaking out of the room.

When I come down the stairs, Saint is watching TV. He turns it off and gets to his feet when he sees me. Things are getting serious now.

"He's asleep." I yawn. "You can check."

Saint taps his jaw. "I believe you."

"Cool. Delete the photos now." I put my hands on my hips. I can't cower, even if he's a good foot taller than me. He slouches to be on the same level as me. I refuse to find that attractive. Saint Cross is a walking nuclear bomb who can draw me into his dangerous, privileged world and spit me out scarred.

I have heard the stories. He goes through women like I go through mints. A lot of girls he slept with dropped out of college. There were rumors that his dad had something to do with it. He has a clear type, though—slim, blonde, and stupid with fake tan and big tits. Thank goodness I don't fit that profile. I'm too curvy to be considered attractive and my skin is naturally brown. My boobs are real, too.

That's why I'm shocked when he stalks toward me. I inch

backward. The tension between us is palatable. My throat moves to swallow as he takes one step, then another, pushing me until my back hits the wall and he's a hair's breadth away from me.

He leans in, his nose on level with mine. His lips are so close. They're so pink and beautiful with a defined cupid's bow. Up close, his godly beauty is unavoidable. I was stupid to let my guard down when he told me about his family. He's not a good guy with a sad past. He's a wolf with sharp fangs. And I'm his prey.

His blue eyes resemble clouds before a thunderstorm, crackling with malevolent electricity. "Did you think it would be easy to get away from me?"

I roll my eyes. I'm sweating under my T-shirt but there's no way I'm dropping my tough girl act. It's the only shield I have against him. "What do you want? Should I get on my knees and beg?"

"If you were kneeling, I'd want you to do more than beg." A dark smile graces his picture-perfect face. Only truly evil people look sexy when they're threatening you. The sexual innuendo makes me shiver. Half in fright and half in anticipation. Will he really force me to get on my knees and suck his cock? Is that what he wants?

Is that what I want?

The spot between my thighs feels unbearably hot. I didn't think I could get aroused by a guy having power over me. But here, in his kingdom, with his brother asleep and just the two of us caught in a web of sexual tension, being trapped with him fuels a dark desire in my core. I want to be caged by his sinister charm and pulled into the underworld where pleasure and pain are equally intense.

My pulse jumps when he leans closer.

"Take whatever you want from me but delete those pics."

My voice sounds throaty and way too sexual. I have no control over my body. I'm under his dark, depraved spell, submerged by his captivating aura.

Saint's jaw tightens. "You don't fucking know what you just asked for."

When I part my lips to retort, his mouth crashes down on mine. I knew it was coming. I knew it the moment anger flashed across his features and my muscles clenched in response. I wanted him to end the sexual heat pulsing between our bodies, to put us out of our misery.

Now I'm scared. My bully's lips move over mine brutally. He sucks on my bottom lip, exerting his dominance. He punishes me with his teeth, biting my plump bottom lip, taking me without caring about my comfort. Instead of agony, all I feel is a heady burst of ecstasy. Nobody has kissed me like this. Nobody has kissed me, period.

When I try to push him away, he grabs my arms and twists them around, pinning them to the wall. My blood heats, rushing to my head. His strong fingers cage my wrists until I stop struggling. His mouth is melded to mine, giving me pricks of pain mixed with waves of pleasure.

He's not letting me get away. I'm his prisoner. My backside pushes into the wall when he squeezes my hips and rakes his fingers over my soft stomach. Sparks flutter under my skin, igniting a fire in my core.

My body is burning up like I have a fever.

His tongue pushes into my mouth. He marks every corner of my me with his ferocious hunger. His teeth graze at my lips. He sucks hard, drawing a moan from me. I hold onto his shoulders to keep my trembling legs from giving out. This is way too intense for a kiss. We're roughly fucking each other with our mouths.

Hate, desire, and passion fuel us. I fight him even as I cling to his muscular shoulders, loving how his masculine strength feels under my fingers. He cups the back of my head. He twists his fingers in my hair, pulling me closer to him. He devours me. My pussy is leaking like a faucet, desperate for more.

My lungs can't take it anymore.

I pull back, needing air. But my bully doesn't let me go.

Saint digs his nails into my neck, possessive until the last second. Then he releases me. I stare at him, panting.

I'm breathless. I have no words. My body is buzzing with electricity. I'm three seconds from grinding against my bully, spreading my legs for him, and letting him have his way with me.

I hate to admit it, but I'm wet for Saint Cross. For my bully.

My lips sting from the impact of that life-changing kiss.

Saint looks satisfied but not happy. Then again, I've never seen the guy smile. He plucks his phone from his pocket and deletes the photo he took.

"Done." He grins, triumphant.

I don't thank him. I just run. My legs are shaky and my mind is in disarray. I bolt out of his opulent townhouse.

THREE

Jennifer

I HATE GOING HOME. The reason I live with my mom is to save on rent and living expenses. My heart races as I take the stairs two at a time. I wish I could turn back, return to Saint's place, and feel his hands resting on my hips, tangling wildly in my hair.

I groan. I must be going crazy. His seduction game is strong. No wonder he gets whoever he wants. He made me feel special, desired, and womanly when he kissed me. But I'm not special. I'm an unattractive middle-class girl hoping for a better future while living in a minefield. He showed me an illusion, a life I could never have. And I fell hook, line, and sinker for it.

I key in the code and enter my apartment.

My body stiffens when I hear the sound of male laughter the moment I walk in. My mood sours as soon as I lay eyes on a middle-aged man in a dirty T-shirt and ripped jeans sitting on the couch, his arm drawn around my mom's shoulders.

Tony is here again. The leech. I almost wish I could have stayed at Saint's place, surrounded by luxurious décor and his cute brother. What I wouldn't give for a better home environment.

I tiptoe around the couch quietly. I don't need attention. My breasts have been sore since a while ago. My lips are swollen from Saint's rough kiss. Embers of heat still burn bright in my belly. My pussy hasn't stopped squeezing. I hate to admit that I'm attracted to the worst guy in college.

Heat sizzles under my skin when I replay the kiss in my head. I touch my lips. Even a soft brush is enough to make my body respond. When I drag my fingertip over the spot he bit, it has me craving more.

Saint Cross is more dangerous than I imagined. I can't afford to be another notch on his bedpost, another girl who fell for his bad boy charm and was discarded after one night. I have a bright future ahead of me. I graduate in eleven months. There's no time for heartbreak.

I pause a bit too long. The man on the couch turns his head backward. His beady eyes lock on me like he has found his target.

"Hello, Jennifer." Tony's tone drips malice and a sense of superiority. He watches me track across the living room, making a beeline for my bedroom. His face is pale and sallow, and his features are indistinct under all the fat. He's a beefy, unattractive man with no redeeming qualities. I have no idea what my mom sees in him. "Looks like you're working hard."

"Unlike you," I reply, scorn dripping from my voice. "Not all of us get to mooch off a gullible woman."

"Jennifer!" My mom shots. "Don't talk to Tony like that. Where are your manners?"

I know better than to argue with her. She's a fool when it comes to Tony. Since he entered our lives two years ago, it has been downhill. She has been giving him money all the time. That's the cash she promised to put toward my college tuition. There's a reason I've had to pick up multiple part-time jobs.

Mom is a successful hotel manager while Tony is trash who has never held a job for longer than six months. But no matter how much I tell her to leave him, she won't. He has a hold over her.

I sigh, leaving the two of them alone and slamming the door to my room shut. Mom has terrible taste in men. My dad was a workaholic, so she divorced him, only to end up with someone worse. At least my biological dad had a good job and made enough to support us. He has a new family now, and he doesn't talk to me.

I open my laptop and place it on my table. It's time to study. Education is the only way I'll get out of this home.

I'm tired of Tony and Mom. She's too stupid to figure out he's a user. I feel threatened and unsafe any time he's near. I doubt she'll protect me even if he did something to me. I only have myself to count on.

My wallet falls open. I see the dollar bills within and my thoughts return to Saint.

I groan. I should never have caught his attention. Now he's digging into my study time, making it impossible to focus.

I pull out my phone, hoping he'll have sent a message apologizing for kissing me. But there's nothing in my inbox.

I guess Saint Cross doesn't have regrets.

THE NEXT DAY, my breasts are sore when I wake up. I examine myself in the bathroom mirror while I shower, noting that my nipples are darker and puffier. My tits are engorged, swollen like there's something inside them. When I squeeze my breasts, a sharp stab of pain trickles through my nerves.

Damn, I don't know if I'm coming down with the flu or if this is just PMS.

I throw on my clothes and quickly head for college. Unfortunately, Saint is in my first class. He smirks at me as I walk in.

"You left in a hurt yesterday. I didn't even get to say goodbye." His sexy lips work into a smile. There's no hint of remorse in his voice, only a teasing note.

I can't make a big deal of the kiss or I'll look like a loser. So I keep my face impassive. "Thanks for deleting the pic."

As I walk away from him, Saint reaches for my wrist. His grip is strong and powerful. When I try to shake him off, he doesn't budge. "I'm still talking."

"Our arrangement is over," I bite out. I hate to admit how much his touch affects me. My pulse is jumping like a racehorse. That familiar, ache between my thighs is back again, making my pussy heavy with desire. My forbidden lust grows stronger every minute. It's like a physical entity inside me.

"It isn't," Saint replies. "You've caught my attention. I want to play with you a little longer."

"I'm not your toy, Saint."

"I'm not asking you to do it for free." Saint hesitates. His eyes darken. "I need a date for my house party. I'll pay you if you come."

"You're paying me to be your fake date?" My jaw hangs in surprise. Of all the things I thought could happen, this wasn't one of them. "Why does the most popular guy on campus want to pay for a date? You could have any girl you want."

"I want you," he replies, with no pause.

I'm about to call him out on his bullshit when a massive wave of pain grips my chest. I draw back. Lines bracket Saint's mouth as he focuses on me. If I didn't know him better, I'd say he was concerned for me.

"What is it?" he asks.

"It's nothing. My boobs hurt. I must be close to my period."

I massage my tits afraid the pain is a sign of cancer or something. I gasp in shock as my nipples tingle, then release a liquid. The liquid soaks my bra, painting two wet spots on my chest. What in the world is happening? What is coming out of my nipples?

"Fuck," I say. "What is happening?"

Saint's eyebrows pull together in a deep furrow. "By any chance, did you drink the green juice at my place last night?"

I press my lips, wondering whether I should lie. No. That would make me seem guilty. He'll take advantage of any psychological vulnerability. "Yeah, I was thirsty. What about it?"

He releases a low, long exhale. "It was my stepmom's. It's a special drink that induces lactation. That must be why your breasts hurt. Your body is producing breastmilk."

"Breastmilk?" I croak, disbelieving.

I groan. Oh god. This is embarrassing. The last thing I need is to be producing breastmilk at this age. I'm not even pregnant.

"You know, it's the nutritious liquid that comes out of your boobs to feed babies." Saint is barely suppressing his grin. He's enjoying seeing me dazed and out of control.

"Your mom is still breastfeeding your brother?" I ask, wincing. I shouldn't judge. Maybe she wants the best for her child. I can't blame her for that.

Saint clears his throat. He's always cold and confident but I see a crack in his mask. "Not my brother. The dean."

"Excuse me? Did you just say she's breastfeeding the dean? The dean is in his fifties."

"It's a kink, Jennifer. A lot of men are turned on by the idea of drinking a woman's breastmilk. Some like seeing milk even if they don't consume it." Saint's face is alarmingly neutral as he explains. I'd have expected him to be blushing but I suppose Saint Cross is comfortable with sex and all kinds of kinks. There's a glint in his eyes.

I don't even want to know how Saint knows all this. He's a guy worth fearing if he can dig up such intimate details about other people's lives.

I close my eyes when a wave of pain passes over my breasts. The tingling in my nipples is getting worse. It's going to be a nightmare if I start dripping milk. "When will it go away?"

"I'm not sure. In a few weeks?"

"Weeks?" I scowl.

"Don't worry. I can help you."

"Help me how?"

"I can make the pain go away. I have a way." He clears his throat. "But in return, you have to act like my date on the day of my house party. I'll buy you an outfit; don't worry."

I hiss. It's not like I have a choice here. I need my breasts to stop leaking. How can I attend college while I'm dripping breast milk?

"Fine," I reply. "So what's your secret method?"

"You can't take back what you said." Saint grabs my hand, dragging me away from my classroom.

Panic seizes my chest. The class starts in a few minutes. I can't miss this lesson. "Where are we going? We have a class to attend."

"Forget about the class. What's more important?"

I bite my bottom lip. I close my eyes. The friction generated by my bra rubbing against my sensitive areolae is driving me crazy. Every time the fabric rubs against my swollen tits, a sharp burst of heat pricks my pussy.

I don't know why but I'm turned on by having my lactating

breasts stimulated. My arousal heightens as the scent of Saint's perfume fills my nostrils, reminding me that a virile, gorgeous man knows my forbidden secret.

I don't protest when Saint pulls me into the men's washroom and locks the door. I don't even complain when he pulls up my top and unclasps my bra, allowing my breasts to spill free.

"Damn, you have nice titties." There's naked lust and reverence in his gaze. He studies my leaking tips. I look down at the stark white lines of breastmilk as they gush over my dark brown areolae.

For some reason, I feel beautiful, like a milky goddess. I've always wanted to have kids but I never imagined having milk in my tits would be such a sensual experience. My chest feels heavy but the heaviness is pleasant. It reminds me of my feminine fertility.

I watch streams of milk spill from my big nipples, collecting over my stomach.

"It hurts, doesn't it?" Saint's fingers feel soothing as they brush over my distended nipples. My pussy clenches, throbbing for more. "Let me make it better, babygirl."

Babygirl. A shudder sizzles through my pussy, hitting me straight in my G-spot. Moisture pools between my legs, soaking my panties. With a single whispered endearment, Saint turns me into a mindless slut. Heat washes through my body, erasing my common sense.

I push my breasts to his mouth. "You want to taste these tits?"

Our gazes meet in a brief, tense encounter.

"There's only one way to end your pain and that's by sucking all the milk out," Saint replies.

I whimper, cupping the back of his head and moving his head closer to my leaking tip. His hair is soft against my fingertips, a rare luxury I allow myself. Touching Saint ignites turbulent emotions in me. I'm scared, yet thrilled. It feels like I'm holding something that could never be mine. "Do whatever you must. But I'll kill you if you tell anyone about this."

"Trust me, that's the last thing I plan to do." Saint kisses my hard nipple. A cold, slow surrender inches down my spine, meeting the inferno in my groin. "Your milky tits are our secret. I'm the only one who will put my mouth on these beauties. You're mine now, Jennifer."

He seals his hot, wet mouth around my aching flesh, swallowing my boob. When he sucks hard, electric shocks jerk through my system. My letdown hits, filling his mouth with fresh breastmilk.

He moans around my breast, devouring the cream I pour into his throat. The erotic sound gets my pussy wetter.

Sparks swell against my wet sex as I drag it back and forth against the hardness of his thigh, needing the rough scrape of my panties against my clit.

My clitoris is swollen from needing sex, from needing my bully to touch me and bring me dark pleasure.

I continue grinding myself on his thigh like a whore, letting him feed on my breasts as I chase my own release against his leg. Every brush, every drag floods my core with liquid rapture. My veins thrum with taboo excitement.

I'm giving myself to a man who holds my life in his hands. The power difference between us should be enough to scare me. He has everything and I have nothing. He could destroy me, leave me with ashes.

Yet, that's what turns me on. I can surrender to him, to his filthy mouth and dirty deeds, knowing I couldn't help it. Knowing he was too powerful for me to resist.

Saint's tongue teases my hard nipple, circling my milky bud. I supply him with more titty milk. The pain in my breasts bleeds away, replaced by a racing heartbeat. When he flicks his tongue against my leaking blood, the most exquisite rapture grips my brain. My nervous system become numb, too numb to feel anything but the electric currents from his tongue flicking against my breast.

He pushes my back against the wall, caging me with his arms as he takes control of my body. He drains one breast and eagerly grasps the other.

"Fuck, you just keep leaking." He bites my other nipple. I close my eyes, clenching my pussy as his sharp teeth saw at my sensitive boob, leaving a trail of fire in their wake. The pain makes sharp pinpricks of heat explode in my groin.

My hips surge forward. My clit throbs, my pussy tightening with desperation as I rub up and down his knee, so close to coming. My folds are slick. My pussy juices run down my thigh.

"Please...keep sucking me," I beg. "Your mouth feels so good."

"You're a pretty little whore, aren't you? Begging to have your titties sucked." Saint squeezes my breast. Milk pours for him as my milk ducts feel the sting of his forceful touch.

"No...I..." Breath deserts my lungs. "I need you, Saint."

My body betrays me, seeking his tongue, longing for his lips to press into my swollen nipple. I eagerly feed him more of my boob.

He drinks from me, guzzling every stream of thick cream. Pleasure jerks in my belly. My body feels disoriented from being pleasured so thoroughly. I cling to Saint's shoulder, seeking his stability. Needing him to provide me a sense of balance because I'm careening down a slope that leads to ruin.

Pressure hums deep in my belly. Tension coils into a tight ball, pulling tighter every time Saint milks me roughly, his teeth scratching my delicate flesh.

I continue pushing myself up against his leg. Friction lashes at my sensitive folds, pushing me toward the finale.

When Saint pulls at my tit with his teeth, demanding everything I have, I lose myself in a frenzy of wild abandon.

My world shatters as the bathroom fades from view, replaced by a galaxy of glittering stars. Cold, white tiles are painted over by a lush, sensual feeling coiling through my groin, radiating to every part of my body. I see golden light shimmering in front of me. My brain is empty. I'm drowning in sensations that swallow my nerves, and make it impossible to feel anything but the expanding ecstasy that envelops my body.

My legs tremble, shaking from the force of that orgasm. I've never come like this. And Saint didn't even have to touch me.

He pulls his mouth away, licking his lips. His saliva on my tits is the only proof of what we did here.

"I completely drained your tits, babygirl. Fuck, your milk was sweet. Are you feeling better?"

I nod, too humiliated to form a response.

"I can help you anytime you want." He winks. "Just text me."

"And what do you want from me in return?"

"You," he says without hesitation. "At my beck and call. It's only fair if I'm going to be at yours."

I sigh. "Whatever. But if you ask me to be your dog, I'll quit."

He laughs. "You have a crazy imagination, Jennifer."

He takes my hand in his. His touch makes me feel vulnerable. What we shared wasn't something superficial. He drank my breastmilk, for Chrissake. And I let him. Not just that, I sought more from him. His touch, his hardness, his passion.

Saint Cross can never know that I orgasmed from him suckling on my breasts.

FOUR

Saint

I can't stop thinking about her milk.

The way it tasted—sweet, warm, fucking decadent. The way it poured from her swollen tits like she was made to feed me. Her breathless moans, her whimpers, the way she ground on my thigh while I suckled her like a starved man.

I've had girls on their knees. I've had girls beg, cry, scream for it.

But Jennifer? She let me drink from her tits like I owned her. And then she came just from that.

No fingers. No cock. No words.

Just my mouth on her leaking breasts and her hips riding my thigh like she was desperate for me to ruin her.

And fuck, did I want to.

Still do.

It's been a day. One long, torturous day. And every time I see her across the quad, or walking down the hallway with that stack of books in her arms, I get hard. Every time I picture the wet spots on her bra, the creamy trails glistening on her chest, my cock twitches like a fucking pervert.

What's worse?

I think she liked it.

Scratch that—I *know* she liked it.

My cock is tense and hot in my jeans. I'm throbbing for her, waiting for any sign that she'll let me fuck her tight cunt. I bet she has never been with a guy who could make her come before. She looked dazed and star-struck when I kissed her, even more so when she orgasmed after rubbing her needy pussy against my thigh like a bitch in heat. She can pretend to be the model student, but she's hiding a filthy mind and a filthier body under that act.

I finally see her in our shared econ lecture. She slips into the room, quiet, her hair tied up, wearing a soft sweater that hugs her tits just enough to make my knuckles itch. She's early. Always is.

I slide into the seat beside her.

She stiffens.

Good.

I lean in, voice low, just for her. "Did you leak for me again last night?"

She jerks away like I burned her.

But she doesn't say no.

Her cheeks flush that perfect shade of pink, and it hits me low—pure, animal hunger. My dick presses against my zipper.

I want to pin her to the desk. Rip her sweater open. See if her nipples are wet again.

Instead, I chuckle, pull out my notebook like I actually give a shit about this class. Jennifer looks anxious sitting next to me. She arcs her head, catching the idiots chattering behind our back. She curls her fingers over her sweater, gathering the thick fabric. There's a lot of whispering going on and I have no doubt a lot of it involves me sitting next to her.

"You shouldn't be sitting with me. Your friends are already missing you." There's the slightest barb in her voice, a sign of her sass.

"Let them miss me," I say. "I do what I want."

She hisses, rolling her eyes. She looks hot doing it. I like her when she has an attitude, when she's playing hard to get. I've never sought the thrill of the chase but Jennifer could change my mind. "Saint, I don't want to be the center of attention. It makes me uncomfortable. The last thing I need a bunch of rich girls threatening me after class because I happened to sit with their crush. So get lost."

"They'd never do that," I assure her, taking the opportunity to press my hand over hers.

"Have you wondered why most of the girls you sleep with are never seen again?"

She holds my gaze. I've never spared a single thought to a girl I fucked once I finished fucking her, but there might be some logic to Jennifer's statement.

The fact I even consider leaving her side so she doesn't get bullied by the girls in our class makes me wonder why I care so much about her. I already milked her. I tasted the forbidden cream in her breasts. I should be over her already. I've had my fun humiliating her, making her squirm. Usually, this is point where I move on. Find a fresh, new woman to fuck.

But I can't seem to do that. Jennifer is stuck in my brain. The last thing I want to do is forget about her. She haunts my thoughts constantly. And my dick craves her cunt.

I need more of her, both sexually and in other ways.

"I'll leave if you ask nicely." I shove my hands into my pockets. "We need to be clear about who is the boss here."

Jennifer parts her lips, her jaw twitching with irritation.

But she schools her features quickly. "Please, oh great Saint, would you do me the honor of getting up from the seat beside me?"

I snort out a laugh. Can't believe Jennifer just said that. She can be funny when she wants to be.

"Since you're asking so nicely, how can I refuse?"

I get to my feet, skipping to the last row of seats in the lecture hall. It's my usual spot and once again, I'm surrounded by the regular group of social climbers and gold diggers, waving their shiny blonde ponytails in my face.

Yet, my attention is fixed on Jennifer.

She might be my toy, my newest curiosity, a puzzle I want to crack, but she's also someone I'm drawn to in a way I can't explain.

A muscle jumps in my jaw when a nerdy-looking guy in glasses saunters over to the seat I just vacated.

You know the type. Flannel. Glasses. Lives for Excel spreadsheets and overpriced fountain pens. He's got that eager look—like he just discovered porn and thinks he's emotionally mature enough to handle real women.

He mutters something to Jennifer and she smiles. I bet he's her usual type, timid and boring.

But everything about him, from his eagerness to the way his gaze keeps dipping to Jennifer's chest annoys me.

Nerd boy clearly has plans and if I have something to say about it, those plans will never materialize.

He does an awkward job at seduction, cracking some pointless joke he read somewhere. I see red when Jennifer laughs. The beautiful, resonant note of her laughter sticks in my belly like a sore reminder of the gulf between us. She doesn't trust me or let her guard down around me. Yet she opened up to Nerd Boy so easily.

I feel my knuckles itch.

She shooed me away, only to give Nerd Boy an opportunity at trying to get into her pants. I get her glares, her curses, her flinches. I get her soaked panties and tear-filled eyes. But not that soft, natural smile. Not the kind that looks like it costs nothing and means everything.

I want to punch the guy's teeth in.

Instead, I grip my pen so hard it snaps in half.

Something primitive wakes up in me. Something dark. Ugly. Possessive. It's a feeling I've never felt before. It churns in the pit of my stomach, making me nauseous.

If I didn't know better, I'd say it was jealousy. But why the fuck would I be jealous of a nerd?

When Jennifer tucks a strand of hair behind her ear and he leans closer, I know the answer.

It's because she might give him something she'll never give me.

And I want to take every part of her.

I saw her first. That means she's mine.

LATER, I find her in the library.

She's curled up near the corner window, headphones in, surrounded by books. Acting like she doesn't know what she did. Like I didn't see her giggling with Nerd Boy while my blood boiled in my veins.

I stalk toward her, slow, deliberate, calculating.

When I reach her table, I drag the chair out next to hers and sit. She looks up and tugs one earbud out, brows lifting.

"What?" she asks, flat and annoyed. "Why're you here?"

I lean back. "You like nerds now?"

She blinks. "Excuse me?"

"That guy in class. The one who looked like he jerks off to calculus. You were all giggles and big eyes."

She narrows her gaze. "He's nice."

"Nice is boring."

"Maybe I like boring."

I grin, but there's no humor in it. "You don't. You like danger. You like getting your tits sucked in bathroom stalls, remember?"

Her lips part, but no sound comes out.

Got her.

I lean forward, lowering my voice to a husky growl. "Want to relive that moment? You can sit on my lap and I'll squeeze those leaking tits until they're dry."

She goes pale, then pink.

I reach under the table, daring to slide my hand over her thigh. Her skin feels like sin and I don't want to stop grazing her creamy flesh. There's something about being near her. She's comforting like a warm bowl of soup. I wonder what it'd feel like to rest my head on her bountiful breasts and feel her warmth against my cheek. Jennifer doesn't have any agenda. She's not hatching schemes to get close to me or marry into the Cross family. I don't feel the need to be wary around her. It's a weight off my chest. Being with her is easy. Maybe that's why I keep seeking out her company, even when I know things between us are complicated.

I'm using her secret to make her obey me. I'm bullying her, using the power difference between us to my advantage.

"You don't belong with guys like him, Jennifer," I whisper, "You belong with someone who knows your body better than you do."

Her jaw tightens. "I'm trying to work."

"So work." I pull my hand back, but not before letting it

graze her inner thigh. "Sitting in the library all evening? You've been here for hours."

"So?"

"So, I'm curious." I tilt my head. "Why spend so much time here? You afraid to go home?"

That stops her.

She blinks at me like I just cracked open something she didn't even know was locked.

I grin, knowing I hit a nerve. When she was babysitting my brother, I noticed a reluctance in her. A haunted look in her eyes that suggested something was going on. The girl has more secrets than I have bank accounts.

"Is that why you're always the last to leave campus?" I ask, quieter now. "Because you'd rather rot here with crusty books and stale coffee than go back to whatever hellhole you call home?"

Jennifer looks down.

Then, after a pause, she says it.

"My mom's boyfriend is always around."

She doesn't look up as she continues. "Tony. He's... he's an alcoholic who mooches off my mother. Says weird things. Stares when my mom's not looking. Once he came into my room without knocking. Just stood there like he was checking me out. I keep the door locked now."

A thick silence wraps around us.

I stop breathing.

There's a pressure in my chest, like something primal is fighting to claw its way out.

"You live with that piece of shit?" I snarl.

She shrugs one shoulder. "I don't have anywhere else to go."

I grip the edge of the table so hard it creaks. A flurry of thoughts pass through me but they're all incinerated by the boiling rage that tears through my system. Jennifer lives with a fucking pervert. That's not even safe. I knew she had it bad, but I had no idea it was this bad.

Tenderness blooms in my chest. I'm too angry to even decode why I'm so mad. I never get attached to my playthings. I have fun with them, have fun fucking them. Then it's goodbye.

I can't even fathom the next sentence that leaves my lips. "I could get rid of him."

Her eyes widen. Her chest rises higher as she fills her lungs with a deep breath.

"What?"

"I could make him disappear."

"You're crazy," she snaps.

The darkness in the pit of my belly roils at her words. I'm proud of being crazy.

I smile, slow and dark. "You let me suck your milk like a hungry baby, and now I'm the one who's crazy?"

Her mouth opens, then closes.

"I'll get rid of him," I say again, voice flat and sharp. I never help people. That's...not me. So I have to throw in some kind of a catch, to make sure she doesn't forget about the power dynamics between us. The subtle control I have over her. "But you'd have to pay the price."

Jennifer doesn't speak. Her lips tremble.

I lean in. "Become mine. For real. Be my slave. My toy. Do everything I say, when I say it. And I'll make Tony vanish."

She stares at me.

And then, she says the one word I hate most.

"No."

I laugh, but there's no humor in it.

"Why the hell not?"

"Because if I let you fix my problems, I'll owe you. I'll *belong* to you."

"You already do."

She stands, ready to bolt.

But I grab her wrist—not hard. Just enough to make her stop.

Her eyes flick to mine.

I see fear there. But also trust. Curiosity. Need.

And fuck, it makes my chest ache.

I let go.

She walks out without saying another word.

I sit there, staring at the empty space she left behind.

I want to kill Tony.

I want to put Jennifer in a castle and never let anyone look at her again.

I want to suck her tits dry and fuck her into compliance.

But more than anything—I want to understand why I *care*.

She's just a girl. A curiosity. A poor little puzzle in tight jeans and leaking tits.

She should be a passing fancy. I shouldn't even bother about her family situation.

So why the fuck can't I stop thinking about what she said?

I'm shaken from my thoughts by a loud crash.

Thunder cracks.

I hear it right after the door slams shut behind Jennifer.

Then lightning flashes, bright enough to cast her retreating silhouette on the wet pavement outside the library. A second later, the sky opens up and the rain starts—cold, punishing, and relentless.

Of course she didn't bring an umbrella.

Of course she's too stubborn to wait it out.

Fucking Jennifer.

I rise from my chair and stalk to the window, watching her dart across the courtyard like a soaked little stray with something to prove. Her sweater clings to her back, transparent with rain. She's trying to be brave. Tough. Like she's not half-wrecked from everything she just told me.

And maybe I should let her go. Let her learn the hard way.

But I can't.

I grab my keys.

I CATCH up to her just as she reaches the edge of the parking lot. She's crossing the grass barefoot—heels dangling from her fingers, hair plastered to her face. She looks like a fucking fever dream: wild, furious, and soaking wet. I want to kiss her sense-less in the rain, warm up her cold body with the passion that's always simmering between us.

"Jennifer!" I shout over the storm.

She ignores me.

I jog to her, water soaking into my sneakers, and catch her elbow. She jerks away, but I don't let go.

"Jesus, are you trying to get struck by lightning?"

"What do you want, Saint?" she snaps. "Here to suck more secrets out of me?"

I grin, but there's no heat behind it. "I came to offer you a ride. You know, like a decent human being."

"You're not a decent anything."

I laugh. "Touché. But I'm still your best option unless you want to catch pneumonia."

She tries to pull away again. I block her path.

She stares up at me, rain sliding down her cheeks like tears. Her lashes are spiky and wet, her lips red from the cold.

God, she's beautiful.

I force my voice into something cruel, something easy. "Don't flatter yourself. I don't care if you die out here. I just don't want you showing up to my house party looking like a drowned rat."

Her eyes narrow. "Your what?"

"Party. My place. Remember? That was our deal when I sucked your pretty titties."

She swallows uncomfortably. "I'll be there. You can leave now"

I grab her wrist before she can twist away from me. She really needs to stop running because it only makes me want to chase her more. "Not so fast. I think I told you that you'll need to act like my girlfriend."

"You want me to be the laughingstock in front of your friends?" She snorts. "I never said I'll do it."

"Then you don't mind if I leak your little lactation secret to the entire campus with a single group chat?" I step closer, watching her chest rise. "You forget—I've had your milk in my mouth. Pretty sure that makes me your god now."

Her nostrils flare, but she doesn't deny it.

"You'll be my date," I continue, "but you're not wearing one of your charity-sale cardigans or whatever depressing shit you normally pick out."

"You mean my clothes from *working* two part-time jobs and *not* having a billionaire daddy?" she snaps.

I smirk. "Exactly. You're playing a part, Jennifer. My date. My arm candy. Nobody's going to believe you belong with me if you show up in one of those tragic Goodwill specials."

She bristles.

"And if I say no?" she bites out.

"Then don't show up at all. But that would be a shame." I pause, voice softening just enough to slide under her skin. "Because I was gonna buy you something real pretty. Something tight. Something short. Something I can unzip with my teeth when the party's over."

Her cheeks flush, even in the cold.

"I hate you," she breathes.

"Get in the car."

"I said no."

Lightning flashes again. Loud. Angry.

I lean closer, voice low. "What's the real reason you won't get in my car? Afraid of what you'll feel when we're alone? Or afraid I'll find out how much you want to be alone with me?"

She's shivering now. Her arms wrapped tight around herself, her eyes flicking toward my SUV parked at the curb.

"I'm not doing this with you," she mutters.

I sigh, dramatic. "Fine. Die wet and cold. See if I care."

I turn to walk back. One... two... three—

"Wait."

I look back.

She's standing there, soaked to the bone, shoulders tight.

"I'm only getting in because I don't want to ruin my laptop," she says, lifting her bag slightly. "Don't make it into something it's not."

I grin as I unlock the doors. "Whatever helps you sleep at night, baby girl."

She climbs in.

And I swear, for a second, the thunder outside is quieter than the storm she just stirred up in me.

FIVE

Saint

THE BASS THUMPS, vibrating the crystal chandelier that hangs from the high ceiling of my townhouse. Bodies grind against each other, moving in sync with the beat. The air is thick with the scent of expensive perfumes and the clink of glasses filled with top-shelf liquor. Everywhere I look, there's a familiar face—the hockey team captain, the head cheerleader, the student body president. Anyone who's anyone at Fall Creek College is here, under my roof.

I lean against the banister, surveying my kingdom with a smirk. My friend, Quinn, sidles up next to me, a beer in his hand and a sneer on his lips. "Another legendary party, Saint. Too bad you'll be going home alone. Again."

I arch an eyebrow. "Jealous that I don't need to beg for seconds?"

Quinn scoffs. "You might be a sex god, but no woman sleeps

with you twice. They know the score. One night with Saint Cross, then it's adiós, bitch."

I shrug, noncommittal. Quinn's not wrong, but he's not entirely right either. I've had my share of one-night stands, but it's not because I'm incapable of keeping a woman interested. It's because I'm not interested in keeping them. Not until now. Not until her.

As if on cue, the front door opens, and Jennifer steps in. The room seems to hush, the air crackling with an electric charge. She's a vision in the dress I picked out for her—a deep red number that hugs her curves like a lover's caress. The neckline plunges, revealing a tantalizing glimpse of her cleavage, and the hem is short enough to showcase her long, toned legs. Her hair is swept up in an elegant bun, a few tendrils framing her face. She's not just beautiful; she's a fucking masterpiece.

Jennifer's swollen tits look fucking obscene, ripe and full, nearly spilling out of her tight dress. My cock jumps, feeling the effect of being around her. She effortlessly makes my body temperature rise, makes me need things I've never needed.

She's standing in the middle of my townhouse living room, her brown eyes wide and nervous, clutching a little purse like it can shield her from the vultures circling the party. They're everywhere tonight—rich kids in pastel shirts and shiny loafers, girls who smell like privilege and desperation.

I grin, pleased at myself. "I'm so glad I decided to throw this party."

Quinn follows my gaze, his eyes widening as he takes her in. "Who the hell is that?"

I straighten up, a sense of pride and possessiveness surging through me. "She's my girlfriend."

Jennifer's hips sway as she walks, the crowd parting for her. She takes her place beside me, and I swear half the guys at the party have turned to look at her tits. They're huge, round, and definitely filled with milk. I'll have to suck on her ripe nipples later. Her skin glows under the fairy lights strung across the ceiling. Her hair is curled loosely, lips painted a soft nude. She looks like sin served on silver. But she doesn't belong here. And they know it.

"Is this some joke, Saint?" Taylor, whose dad runs a small finance company, frowns at me, popping a beer. "Didn't know you were into the charity case look."

I smile slowly. "You'd know if you spent more time reading the room and less time reading your Instagram comments."

Jennifer stiffens beside me. I can feel the tension in her body like a live wire. I know this is hard for her—being surrounded by rich assholes who think money makes them gods. But she's mine tonight. And I want everyone to see it.

"I guess Saint has decided to hop on the diversity trend." Taylor sneers at Jennifer, studying her with a haughty expression. It irks me that she thinks she has any right to diss my taste in women or to insult Jennifer based on her race. Jennifer is gorgeous and deep, not a shallow rich heiress with no brains. "You must be so proud to date a Cross. But I wouldn't start dreaming of marriage. Eventually, he must marry someone of his caliber."

Jennifer swallows, uncomfortable. "I'm not hoping for a fairytale."

She pulls away from me. My chest feels hollow. I wanted this party to be for her, to show everyone that she's my new queen. Instead, they're all suspicious of her. Given my reputation, they're assuming she's just a one-night-stand.

I let Jennifer go, not wanting her to be derided by this group of vile bastards I call friends. I'm beginning to question my life decisions lately.

The only reason I hang out with these assholes is because their parents will be useful to me in the future. They're all worthless otherwise. They're too self-absorbed to be actual friends. I've known them for years, yet none of them is aware of my stepmother's affair with the dean or my past. I was able to tell Jennifer everything in a single evening. She listened, challenging me with her sass, but never shutting me down. I felt safe with her. I felt seen with her.

That's why I kissed her. I wanted her to know that she'd triggered something in me, something violent and intense. Something she can't run away from.

My phone buzzes. I step away from the loud living room to take the call.

I lose track of her for maybe fifteen minutes while I deal with a supplier for my dad's business on the phone. When I come back, Jennifer is nowhere to be seen.

I scan the crowd. My chest gets tight. Panic rises like smoke in my throat.

Then I see her—slumped on the staircase, her dress wrinkled, her eyes unfocused. A couple of my so-called friends are standing near her, snickering. One of them, Quinn, leans a little too close, his hand ghosting over her bare shoulder.

Something in me snaps.

I charge forward. "Get the fuck away from her."

Quinn turns, eyebrows raised. "Chill, man. We're just talking."

"She can barely stand." I reach for her, and she tries to lift her head but it lolls to the side. My blood ices over. Her pupils are blown, her skin pale. "What did you do to her?"

Quinn laughs nervously. "Nothing, man. Maybe she drank too much—"

I punch him.

It's not a warning shot.

It's a straight, bone-breaking crack across his jaw. He hits the floor with a grunt, groaning, clutching his face as blood trickles from his nose.

"Fuck," someone gasps. "Saint, what the hell—"

"She was roofied." My voice is low. Dangerous. I scoop Jennifer into my arms. Her head lolls against my shoulder. "If I find out who else was involved, they're next."

I carry her upstairs. The party keeps going downstairs. No one dares follow me.

In my room, I lay her on the bed gently. She mumbles something, her lashes fluttering. I pull a blanket over her, but her dress is all wrong. I hate the sight of it now. Like she was put on display. Like I fed her to the wolves.

My jaw clenches as I strip down to my boxers and slip in next to her. Just to make sure she's okay. Just to hold her.

Just to watch the rise and fall of her chest.

"I'm sorry." I breathe into the air. "I didn't want this to happen."

But Jennifer doesn't reply, lost in a world that's far away from mine.

SHE WAKES SLOWLY, sometime after midnight. The party is over. I sent everyone home. I rearranged Quinn's face so he had to be taken away in an ambulance. Of course, he won't press charges. He knows who my dad is. And he knows he fucking deserved it. It was either the hospital or prison. He'll thank me later for saving him from a lengthy and embarrassing court case.

Jennifer's eyes flutter open, dazed and glassy, before locking on me. Her fingers grasp air, before brushing against mine. I sandwich her hand between my palms, savoring the softness of her skin, the smoothness of its texture.

And then she jolts up. She looks around, hair messy, breasts nearly popping out of her dress, eyes heavy-lidded with sleep. She's breathtaking when she's in her natural state. The urge to throw my arms around her nags at me, but I resist. I don't want to scare her after she was roofied.

Her scream is hoarse and short. "What the fuck—why am I here? What did you do to me? Did you...did you..."

A cry leaves her throat. Her voice breaks.

I sit up, my voice calm. "Nothing happened. No one touched you. You're safe."

She scrambles back, clutching the sheet to her chest. "You... You were with me all night?"

"Yes. After I found you roofied and about to be groped by Quinn fucking Hayes. I carried you up here. You've been asleep since."

Her breathing is shallow. Her gaze drops to my bare chest, then darts away. "I thought—" Her voice cracks. "I thought you were the bad guy."

"I'm a bully," I say, voice rough. "Not a rapist."

She looks at me, lips trembling. "I didn't think those two were that far apart."

"They are," I snap. "You think I'd let some frat boy touch you? You think I'd let *anyone* else put their filthy hands on you?"

She blinks, stunned. I lean closer, letting my anger show. "You're mine, Jennifer. Mine to fuck with. Mine to break. Mine to own."

Her lips part. They're so plump and juicy, slick with lip-gloss. She's the perfect midnight temptation with the moonlight curling over her brown skin, pristine sheets draped around her sensual form. She looks ethereal, like an angel who belongs in a different world.

"I'm the only one who gets to watch you fall apart," I say. "And I'll only touch you when you beg me to fuck you."

I expect her to protest immediately, tell me how that'll never happen but she's surprisingly quiet.

Jennifer wiggles her toes, hesitating as she pushes her legs over the bed. Her heels graze the carpet.

"What about the guys who roofied me?" Her eyes speak volumes. My babygirl is scared, terrified of stepping out of here and being assaulted. "Are they still there?"

A bitter snort leaves me. "The party ended a while ago."

"I thought it'd go on longer." Jennifer pulls at a strand of her chocolate brown hair. "Don't these parties usually stretch late into the night?"

"We had to cut it short because I broke Quinn's jaw and he had to be taken to the hospital."

"You did what?"

"I punched him. Hard. He deserved it. He's crazy if he thinks he can rape my girlfriend in my house."

Silence stretches. Her nipples push against the thin fabric of the sheet. Her chest rises, falls, rises. I know that look. She's scared, yes—but also turned on.

The heat between us simmers again.

And I want her. Bad.

But not like this. Not when she's terrified and shaken. I'll have her open, willing, and ready, spreading her legs for me voluntarily.

"Thank you, Saint. You have no idea how grateful I am. You protected me. When you could have left me to...to the wolves." A lone tear trails down her cheek, shimmering like a silver river against the wan light of the moon. "I thought all rich heirs were like that. Callous."

"I'm not the rich guy stereotype you think I am," I say, hoping she'll change her mind about me. I'm tired of her wariness, her lack of trust. I might be literally threatening her into being girlfriend, but she must know that I don't mean any harm.

"I'm sorry for judging you without giving you a chance." Jennifer reaches her hand to wipe away her tear but I beat her to it.

My fingers gather the wetness on her cheek.

"I will always protect you," I murmur, stroking her jaw. "As long as I own you, I will take care of you. I value my possessions."

Jennifer sniffles. "I never thought I'd say this, but I'm glad I'm yours."

She stares at me a beat too long. I can't read her emotions. I don't know if she's mad or relieved. All I know is that she made me do things I never did in the past. I never protected girls. I mean, I never let them get raped, either. But no one aroused my masculine need to be a protector.

Jennifer brings it out of me. The kindness, the cockiness, the forbidden urges. Her delicate, vulnerable body makes me want to keep her under me.

I stand, grabbing a shirt. "Next time someone fucks with you, tell me."

"Why?" she asks, voice quiet.

I pause at the door.

"Because I'll kill them."

Then I leave.

Let her think about what that means.

Let her wonder just how far I'll go.

For her.

SIX

Jennifer

I'M STILL SHAKING.

Hours have passed since I woke up in Saint's bed, and the shame hasn't stopped crawling under my skin. I scrub my hands over my arms like I can erase what happened—what almost happened. Not with Saint. With them.

I remember laughter. Hands. Heat in my chest. A bitter taste on my tongue. Then nothing. Black.

And then... blue eyes. A voice like fire. And him.

Saint.

I want to scream, to cry, to tear off this stupid dress and forget all of it. But instead, I sit frozen in the campus library, pretending to read an accounting textbook while I relive every moment of last night.

He saved me.

He beat someone bloody for me.

And that scares me more than anything.

Because I liked the way it felt. Being protected. Being claimed. Being *his*.

No one has ever fought for me like that. Not my mom. Not my dad. Not anyone.

And now I'm spiraling.

I close the book, shove it into my bag, and rush out of the library like my skin's on fire. The sky is heavy with clouds, the kind that promise a downpour. Thunder rumbles as I walk home, and it feels fitting—stormy skies for a stormy life.

———

I MANAGE to avoid Saint for the next few days. It's easy because I don't run into him on campus even once. I bought a breast pump using the money I made from babysitting Easton. It helps me relieve the ache in my breasts when it's bad. But it's nothing compared to a warm, hungry mouth sucking from me.

Saint opened my eyes to a new realm of pleasure when he milked me. Now every time I touch my puffy breasts, every time I watch milk trickling down my fat mounds, I'm hit with an intense ache in my pussy. I need to be loved while I'm lactating. I want to be fucked while Saint drinks from my breasts, allowing me to nurture him as he destroys my pussy.

I never thought I'd be into weird shit like lactation but .

I wonder how Saint is doing. He must feel guilty for what happened because he hasn't turned up to any of his classes.

A week passes with no messages or word from him. He told me I was his, that I was his fake girlfriend and it felt amazing to be his, even if our relationship was fake. Now I'm left with silence.

That afternoon, as I'm heading to the Bursar's Office, I do the most uncharacteristic thing ever and text him first.

Jennifer: *I hope you're fine. If the reason you're cutting classes is to avoid me, you don't have to worry. I'm over it.*

I stuff my phone in my bag, heart thumping. Why am I being so nice to my bully? Sure, he helped me a few times, once with my breast milk, once with those assholes who tried to take advantage of me at his party. I hate to admit it, but I'm softening toward him.

He seems more human and less monster with every passing day.

He's the most complex human being I know, a study in contrasts. There's depth to his character. He's more than a stereotype, more than what I assumed he was. I'm mesmerized by his deep protectiveness, the natural paternal instinct he shows around Easton, the way he cares for the people he has decided to call his own.

If he were someone different, I'd be open to dating him. But like Taylor said, there's no happy ending waiting for me and Saint. I'm the most unsuitable girl for him. He'll marry someone from upper-crust society, a white girl with no foreign blood in her veins, whose family history can be traced back three hundred years. I'm simply a curiosity, a way to kill time before he graduates. If I'm not careful, I'll end up giving more of myself to him than I ought to.

I stroll into the Bursar's Office. There's no line.

"Hi, I wanted a receipt for my tuition fee payment," I say, handing them my student ID.

The lady gives me look of puzzlement after she enters my details into the system. "I'm sorry your fees have not been paid. It's about to be overdue. Will you require some assistance in figuring out how to pay it?"

"Can you check again. My mom said she'll pay..." I bite my nails. Mom is usually punctual with paying my fees, but she has missed the deadlines once or twice. And on both occasions, it had something to do with Tony.

A knot tightens in my stomach. I don't want to imagine the worst but I can't help it. I've lived in a volatile family environment since my mother's disgusting boyfriend became a part of our life. I know Mom loves me, but it's becoming clearer by the day that she doesn't love me as much as she loves Tony. Even though I'm her flesh and blood. I don't take advantage of her. I was there for her when she left Dad.

But she's the kind of woman who values romance and men more than she values anything else. When Dad cheated on her, it broke her. She lost faith in her attractiveness as a woman. She had grown up watching hyper romantic telenovelas, imagining herself as the heroine. She worked hard to be successful so she could have a good marriage. She only had one kid because she was too busy trying to play the role of the perfect wife, one who provides for the family and cooks for her husband. Tony swooped in on her when she was vulnerable, telling her what she needed to hear, making her feel like he couldn't live without her.

She needed to belong to someone and she took what was available.

"Yes, your fees have not been paid. I checked again," the lady at the counter replies. "I see you're on a scholarship. I'll try and find out if we can lower the amount somehow. Would you like to schedule a meeting with the Bursar's Office. We can discuss options."

I shake my head. "No. I think my Mom just forgot to pay it. I'll remind her."

"Sure. I hope I was of help."

I don't hear her final words. My ears feel numb. My legs feel like lead as I drag myself out of the Bursar's Office.

IT RAINS on the way back. I don't even bother with an umbrella. The somber skies and thick downpour match my mood perfectly.

My shoes squelch as I step into the apartment. The door creaks. A voice I loathe fills the air.

"Hey, chica."

Tony.

He's on the couch again, stinking of cigarettes and cheap whiskey. My mom perches next to him like a broken doll, her eyes hollow. There's a check on the table. My name on it. Or there *was*.

"Where's my tuition money?" My voice is low. Cold. "I was at the Bursar's Office today. They said they've not received my fees for the next term."

My mom won't meet my eyes. Tony chuckles. "I needed the money. My business hit a snag."

"You don't have a business," I hiss. "You have a drinking habit."

"Jennifer," my mother snaps. "Don't be ungrateful."

Ungrateful? I want to laugh and scream at the same time.

I'm drowning. And she just cut off my only lifeline. All I had in life was one dream, one thing that made me push myself out of bed every day. Now I don't know if I'll be able to attend college anymore.

I'm screwed. My own mother screwed me over for a man. And I have no one to talk to, no one to vent to.

"I hope he was worth it," I whisper before turning and slamming the door behind me.

I hurriedly boot up my laptop once I'm in my room. I log into my bank account but the paltry sum in it cannot cover even half my fees. A long sight trails all the way up to the ceiling. I could call my abuela. She lives with my aunt. I could ask them to lend me some money, promise them I'll pay it back. Unlike my mother, they value family. They'd do anything to support me.

But they're not exactly rich. My aunt is a receptionist at a local funeral home. She already struggles to make ends meet. Plus, she has to take care of my grandma, too.

Cold raindrops beat against my window, sinking me into an abyss of negative thoughts. Fear races through me, dragging me away from my room to a somber reality filled with financial struggles. If I can't pay my fees, I'll have to drop out or delay my graduation. I don't want to do either. I want to become financially independent as soon as possible. I plan to move in with my abuela and aunt and help them when I start earning. Mom can fend for herself. She has Tony. It's not like she cares if I'm around.

The sick sound of Tony's laughter and the television rings in my ears, creeping through the door.

I can't stay in my room. I can't hang around that man, knowing all I want to do is strangle him.

I escape my room, escape the house where I feel like a stranger.

The skies outside are cloudy. Lightning flashes through the inky balck sky.

The rain soaks me to the bone as I walk, no plan, no umbrella, no idea what I'm doing. Only one thought pulls me forward:

Saint.

His name is a curse. A drug. A prayer.

I end up outside his townhouse, water dripping from my hair, my dress clinging to my skin. I ring the bell once. Then again. I don't stop until the door flies open.

He's shirtless.

Of course he's shirtless.

His black hair is messy, like he's been running his hands through it. His blue eyes scan me, take in the wet clothes, the broken expression, the trembling hands.

"Shit," he mutters, stepping aside. "Get in before you catch pneumonia."

I stumble inside. His heat hits me instantly. I feel stupid for being here. Weak. But I can't leave.

"I need you to make me forget," I whisper.

He shuts the door.

"What happened?" His voice is quiet. Dangerous.

"Nothing I want to remember." My bottom lip wobbles. "Just... I don't want to think anymore. Please."

For a second, he doesn't move. Then something in him breaks.

"Poor girl," he breathes, stepping forward. He wraps his arms around me. I press my face to his chest, inhale him. Fresh soap. Warm skin. Sin.

He kisses my temple, my cheek, my jaw. "You want to forget? I'll help you forget."

He lifts me—actually lifts me—and carries me up the stairs. His chest is solid and warm as I lean against it. With him, I'm enveloped in comfort and a sense of stability. Saint is a stranger but being with him feels like being home. Like being in an oasis that won't dry up and leave me thirsty.

I never imagined I'd put my emotional well-being in his hands someday, that I'd let him care for me when I was at my weakest.

I sure as hell didn't imagine he'd do it. Anxious emotions tremble in my chest. But when Saint skims his thumb along my arm, it dissolves. My pussy grows hot, drips for the man who is carrying me without questions. Giving me what I need. I might have to pay an arm and leg for this later, but it'll be worth it.

"Whoever put that expression on your face, I wish I could punch his face."

He draws an easy smile from me. "I wish you could, too."

I'd love to see him smack Tony.

By the time we reach his room, I'm soaked, shivering, unraveling. He sets me down gently and peels off my wet dress. My nipples harden under the cold air, and he stares at them like they're fucking holy.

His fingers trail over my collarbone. "Still sore?"

I nod.

"I haven't milked you in days. I'm sorry. I was...I was dealing with something."

I cup his face, sick of denying myself what I want. "I don't care. I want your mouth on my tits now. Please. I can't stand it anymore."

He doesn't hesitate.

He pushes me down on the bed, pulls off his sweatpants, and climbs between my legs. His hands are rough but his mouth is reverent as he suckles me again, drinking the milk that makes my breasts ache. My head falls back.

"Saint..."

He groans. "You taste like heaven."

The pleasure is instant. Sharp. Hot.

His hands trail down, sliding my soaked panties off. He massages my clit with his fingers. I moan as friction caresses my deepest parts with every touch of his fingertips. Desire, cruel and heavy, gnaws at my core.

I scrunch my eyes closing, crying with pleasure as Saint's mouth wraps around my other breast, drawing thick streams of milk from my sensitive boob. His tongue laps against my tender bud. I feel every flick of his tongue deep in my pussy, shaking me from the inside.

Electric sparks erupt as he drags his jaw over my tender

boob. His stubble, sharp and overgrown, bristles against my skin, adding a touch of pain to my milking expeirence. Every time he stimulates my breast, my pussy responds with a hard jerk. My wet walls close around emptiness, needing to be filled.

"Saint..." I utter his name like a prayer.

He toys with my clit, launching a lightning bolt of raw pleasure through my bloodstream. His fingers part my pussy, teasing my slick folds until I close my legs, the stimulation too much to bear. He circles my entrance, my pussy hole, with gentle, barely-there touches. I feel every single one in my belly, punching a hole into my resolve.

Heat detonates in me like an atom bomb, pumping lava through my veins. I can't contain the mass of tension writhing in my groin. He plays with my boobs, using his mouth to extract every sensation I never knew I was capable of.

Saint is indeed a sex god and I'm his captive, willing to give him every part of my soul in return for an earth-shattering orgasm that will carry me away from the ugliness of the world.

His room is a sanctuary. A luxurious place I can't enter with my own means. And he's my solace, my dark knight, my maddest fantasy.

"You said you'd fuck me if I begged. I'm begging." My voice tears through the wet noises of his mouth suckling on my teat. His forceful suction makes my breasts feel intensely drained, intensely devoured.

"Jennifer." A single word, an uncertain response. But it's enough. Because the next moment, I feel his erection pushing against my soft folds. Parting my pussy as he fits himself against my aching hole.

"I'm going to fuck you now," he says, voice like smoke. "No condom. I need to feel all of you."

I should stop him.

I don't.

I spread my legs.

"Do it," I whisper. "Make me forget."

His cock thrusts into me in one slow, devastating stroke.

He's thick. He's hard. He fills me like he was made to.

My back arches. My pussy clenches. My walls wrap around him. He moves inside me, a steady rhythm that brings me peace. That bathes me in tranquility. His chest moves against me, his legs caging mine. He grabs my hips, thrusting harder, moving deeper, hitting my G-spot.

Tonight, I'm his whore, his toy, whatever he wants me to be. And it feels so good, forgetting who I am for a few minutes. Losing myself in the arms of a man who is all-consuming, powerful, and unforgettable.

Saint snarls. "Tight. Fuck, you're milking me already."

He fucks me like a man possessed. Deep, unrelenting strokes. His hand cups my leaking breast while the other grips my hip like he owns it.

"Say it," he demands.

"What?"

"Say you're mine."

I close my eyes. Let go.

"I'm yours."

His rhythm stutters.

Then he growls—and comes inside me, hot and raw and claiming. Cum fills me again and again and he spurts load after load into my unprotected pussy. He paints my walls with semen, making me feel deliciously used.

The trickle of his seed in my fertile depths awakens a forbidden hunger in me. The hunger to be bred, to be heavy with a child. The need to create something I can cherish and protect. I don't even think about the consequences, don't fear them. I surrender to the haze of pleasure that marks my insides.

I'm helpless against my primal feminine need. I accept every drop of cum until my pussy overflows.

I follow seconds later, my orgasm ripping through me like a violent storm.

He collapses beside me, still inside me, still pulsing.

I cry after.

Quietly.

He kisses the tears off my cheeks.

"I've got you now," he whispers.

And I almost believe him.

SEVEN

Jennifer

I'M STARTING to wonder if I've been kidnapped without realizing it.

Because for the third day in a row, I find myself running errands for Saint Cross like it's my full-time job. This time, it's overpriced dog food for his stepmom's Pomeranian and a dry-cleaned blazer that probably costs more than my rent.

The annoying part?

I don't even mind.

Saint texts me a list. No "please." No "thank you." Just commands, one after the other. And I follow them. Like an idiot. Like someone with no self-respect.

But also... like someone who likes being useful to him.

God, I hate myself a little.

But I also kind of hate how *not* hated I feel when I'm around him. And how I've started hanging out at his townhouse more and more, even when he's not threatening to blackmail me or bring up my embarrassingly leaking tits.

The weirdest part?

He's stopped threatening me altogether.

We just... hang out.

I'm mystified at how conversations flow easily between us these days. The banter between us. Is effortless, too. The tension between us is well and alive, but I'm able to relieve my sexual frustrations with a bout of verbal sparring. Saint has a sharp tongue and he doesn't hold back when I provoke him. Oddly, I find that endearing about him.

He's real. After seeing Tony, who makes me sick with how he acts around my mom, then completely changes the moment he's gone, I find Saint's blatant honesty refreshing.

Things shifted between us after we had sex. I feel closer to him and he has definitely softened toward me. He's a bit possessive, though. Anytime I don't text him, he finds another excuse or errand to bring me into his orbit.

My feelings are slowly changing. Saint doesn't feel like my bully anymore. He feels more like a friend. He punched a guy to protect me. He comforted me, and held me through the night after my mother betrayed me.

There's an emotional connection between us. I feel it even when we're apart. I never thought I'd say this but I feel safe with Saint. He has showed me that he might be crazy and intense, but he won't hurt me.

Today, after picking up his stuff, I head to his place and find him sitting on the floor with Easton, building a block tower. He looks up at me like he's been expecting me, like I belong here.

Easton perks up at the sight of me, too. I wave at him. After the babysitting gig, he seems to have warmed up to me. His presence adds a sweetness to Saint's home. Also, as long as he's around, I know Saint won't try anything with me, so there's that, too.

"Are you hungry?" Saint asks his brother.

I sigh inwardly, knowing he's about to send me on another errand.

Easton's eyes twinkle. "I want ice cream."

I pre-emptively groan. Easton tilts his head, puzzled at my response. "I'll go get it," I volunteer, feeling my self-esteem crying. I might as well start wearing a maid outfit and quit college if I'm going to do this.

"No." Saint's deep, growly voice stops me in my tracks before I can spin around and head to the door. "We're going together."

"Yeah!" Easton claps and makes a delighted noise, and I find myself smiling before I can stop it.

"Come on," he says, standing up and grabbing his keys. He casually snakes his arm around me as he leads me out of the door but the gesture feels like a familiar bond between friends rather than something forced. This is another thing that has changed between us.

Since I let him come inside me, I lean into his touch instead of shrugging him off. Physical contact, especially when it's non-sexual makes a thrill fly through my veins. It feels like Saint is treating me as more than his slave. He's treating me like his buddy, like I mean something to him.

I know I'm stupid for believing in such things. I'm different from the girls he has dated before. He's intrigued for now but he'll soon get over me.

I still haven't gone to the campus health center to get on birth control. I let Saint come inside me raw. I could get pregnant but just like I can't bring myself to stop yearning for Saint's company, I can't bring myself to do the right thing and get an IUD, either. I keep putting it off.

"Where are we going?" I ask.

"Ice cream," Easton replies, trailing behind me like a faithful puppy.

Saint opens the door to his SUV. "That's right. We're going to grab some ice cream. You can have some, too, Jennifer."

"Sure, that sounds great." Spring has been slowly moving into summer. It's the perfect season for ice cream. Besides, I can't miss an opportunity for free food.

Fifteen minutes later, we're sitting outside a trendy little creamery with neon signs and cartoon cones painted on the windows. Saint orders chocolate with rainbow sprinkles—for Easton. And pistachio for himself. Apparently, he has an old man's taste in ice cream.

I get strawberry. Classic. Sweet. Predictable.

Saint watches me lick it, and I feel his eyes on my mouth like a physical heat.

"Don't look at me like that," I murmur.

"Why?" he asks, deadpan. "You always eat like that?"

"Like what?"

"Like you're auditioning to suck me off in a Baskin-Robbins parking lot."

My cheeks burn. My pussy weeps moisture. The one thing that hasn't changed is that my pussy still feels hot and needy every time I'm around Easton. His sexual effect on me is insane. And now that I know how well his dick stretches my cunt, I want him even more.

"You're disgusting." I tap the table.

He plants his elbow on the table, smirking. "And you're cute when you blush."

I look away, hiding my smile behind my cone.

Easton babbles something about sprinkles falling on the sidewalk, and Saint leans over to brush the boy's hair back from his forehead. The motion is soft. Natural.

And it kills me.

Because this is starting to feel easy.

Too easy.

Like I'm getting used to the rhythm of being around him. Like I actually like it.

I glance at my bully from the corner of my eye. He's sitting back in the metal chair, legs spread like a king who owns everything he sees. But when he glances at me, there's no cruelty in his gaze. Just something sharp and unreadable. Something that makes my stomach twist.

He knows all my secrets. My mom. Tony. The lactation thing. The way I came from his mouth on my tits without him even touching me between the legs.

And he still wants me around.

More than that—he *lets* me be me. With the sarcasm. The fire. The walls I don't even try to lower. Everybody always made it seem that I wasn't easy to love or even tolerate. I'm curvy, with colored skin and average features. I'm no beauty. My intellect coupled with my tendency to argue exasperates my mom and Tony.

But Saint doesn't flinch when I push back.

He *likes* it.

He savors the verbal sparring between us like it's sweet ice cream. I do, too. I don't often meet someone who can make me laugh or make me think hard to come up with a suitable retort.

"Thanks for the ice cream," I mutter under my breath. "It's good."

One corner of Saint's lips lifts up in a slow, sexy smile. "And here I thought you were incapable of gratitude."

"Shut up," I snap.

Easton pipes up, wedging himself between Saint and me. His eyebrows tense. "Are you fighting?"

"No." Saint caresses his head. "That's how she talks."

I snort, but I can't bite back the smile that threatens to form on my lips. I won't give him the satisfaction of seeing me smile at his words but it's hard. With every passing day, he's crawling under my skin, burrowing his way into parts of me that nobody has accessed before. And I let him take it all, opening myself freely, even knowing the consequences could destroy me.

It's inexplicable. The trust I feel toward him. The need for connection with someone who can understand me.

Saint doesn't look like the brightest bulb in the box but he saw through me. He could tell I was avoiding going home and staying at the library as an excuse. Nobody has paid so much attention to me before. It feels good knowing someone notices me, someone cares for me. He even offered to get rid of Tony, which was extreme, but in the moment, it made me incredibly happy.

It felt like I had an ally. Someone to fight for me.

But my dark knight is more broken and more dangerous than he should be.

As I watch the last rays of sunlight skim the perfect angles of Saint's face, it takes my breath away. The sun is setting. His profile looks stunning against the dusk sky.

I grip my cone too hard, tamping down the urge to run my fingers over his smooth jaw and chiseled nose.

Not today. I won't give in to him again today.

———————

BACK AT HIS TOWNHOUSE, Easton conks out early.

I help bathe him and get him into pajamas while Saint gets his dinner ready. By the time I lay him in the crib, the kid's snoring softly with one hand clutched around a stuffed elephant.

I hover for a moment, brushing my fingers down the boy's cheek, then back away.

In the hallway, Saint is leaning against the wall. Arms folded. Watching me.

"You're good with him," he says.

I shrug. "He's sweet."

"Not everyone thinks so."

"Well, not everyone has taste."

He snorts. "You're in rare form tonight."

"Must be the strawberry."

We head downstairs and collapse on the oversized couch in the living room. For a few minutes, we don't say anything. The air is heavy with something neither of us knows how to name.

Saint turns on the television, then groans at the ceiling when his dad's face flashes through the screen. It's a business channel and they're talking about the new expansion plans and profits that Saint's dad's company made this year. I've never seen Mr. Cross and I'm surprised that he looks different from both his sons. For one, he has gray eyes and he's thin and wiry. Even in a business suit, he looks more like a college professor than professional quarterback.

"You don't like your Dad?" I ask as Saint turns on the television.

"My dad's grooming me to take over the company," he says. "He hasn't said it in so many words, but it's obvious."

I glance at him. "Is that what you want?"

He scoffs. "What I want doesn't matter. It never did."

"That's not true."

He raises a brow. "You don't even know me."

"I know enough."

That seems to rattle him. He frowns. "What do you know?"

I take a breath. "I know you're cruel. And impulsive. And probably a little bit emotionally broken."

He nods slowly, lips twitching. "So far, I'm flattered."

"But I also know you're good to your brother. And that you hate your stepmom. And that you care more than you let on."

Silence.

"You don't want to be your dad," I say softly.

He doesn't answer.

Just stares ahead like he's trying to swallow glass.

"Whatever. Isn't it getting late tonight?" He clears his throat. "I don't want you to accuse me of keeping you here against your will."

And that's when I realize I don't want to go home.

Not tonight. Not back to Tony. Not to the silence, the tension, the feeling of always looking over my shoulder.

"You're not keeping me against my will. I want to stay. My mom won't be back from work until late."

Saint must see the reluctance in my face, because he says, "There are four guest rooms upstairs."

I blink.

"What?"

"You can stay. If you don't want to go back."

"I—" My throat tightens.

"You'll be safe here," he adds, eyes still fixed on the TV. "Nobody will bother you."

I stare at him, my heart aching in a way I didn't expect.

"Thank you," I whisper.

He finally looks at me.

And for once, there's no teasing in his expression. No threat.

Just... kindness. Raw and real.

"Don't get used to it," he mutters.

But I already am.

EIGHT

Jennifer

THE MORNING LIGHT filters through the sheer curtains, casting a soft glow over the elegantly appointed guest room. I blink away the remnants of sleep, momentarily disoriented by the unfamiliar surroundings. Then it all comes rushing back—Saint, the ice cream, the offer to stay the night. I'm safe here, away from Tony's leering eyes and my mom's desperate denial.

I stretch, feeling a sense of peace that's been missing for a long time. The bed is divine, a cloud of comfort that makes me want to burrow back under the covers. But the scent of something delicious wafts through the air, tempting me to explore.

Wrapping a plush robe around me, I pad downstairs, following the aroma. The sight that greets me steals my breath away. Saint, dressed in low-slung sweatpants and a faded tee, is placing dishes on the dining table. The spread is something out of a five-star brunch menu: fluffy pancakes drizzled with syrup, fresh berries glistening like jewels, crispy bacon, and perfectly scrambled eggs. There's even a vase of fresh flowers, adding a touch of elegance.

"Wow," I murmur, taking it all in. "You did all this?"

He turns to me, a smirk playing on his lips. "Don't sound so surprised, Garcia. I'm a man of many talents."

"I see that." I can't help but smile back, feeling a warmth spread through me that has nothing to do with the food.

He pulls out a chair for me, a gentlemanly gesture that feels both natural and unexpected. "Sit. Eat."

I obey, feeling spoiled and cherished. It's a strange sensation, one I could easily get used to. Saint sits beside me, his thigh brushing against mine under the table. He picks up a fork, spears a piece of pancake, and holds it out to me.

"Open up," he teases, his blue eyes dancing with amusement.

I hesitate, then part my lips, allowing him to feed me. The pancake is light and fluffy, the syrup sweet and indulgent

I take another bite, this time from my own fork, but Saint's eyes never leave mine. He watches me like he finds pleasure in my enjoyment, like my simple act of eating is fascinating. I squirm under his intense gaze, but there's nowhere I'd rather be than here, with him.

"This is amazing," I say, gesturing to the spread. "I can't remember the last time I had a breakfast like this."

"Get used to it," he says, winking. "I like my woman well-fed."

I roll my eyes, but my cheeks flush with pleasure. "Your woman, huh?"

He leans back in his chair, a king surveying his kingdom. "You're mine for now. At least until your breasts stop leaking."

My nipples pinch with pain when he mentions my breasts. My tits are engorged, filled with milk. He said I'd stop lactating in a few weeks but my breasts keep filling up with more milk.

Panic trembles through me as I wonder if the reason my breasts are sore and still producing milk is because I might be pregnant.

But I erase the thought, not even wanting to explore the dark possibility.

"And what happens when you get bored of me? When you move on to the next challenge?" I ask, my voice barely above a whisper. I hate myself for ruining the moment, but I need to know. I need to protect myself.

Saint's expression softens, and he reaches out, tucking a strand of hair behind my ear. "Who says I'll get bored? Maybe you're not giving yourself enough credit."

I scoff. "I'm not one of your blondes, Saint. I'm not... I'm not like those pretty princesses who grew up with privileges."

"No, you're not," he agrees, his thumb tracing the line of my jaw. "You're real. You're smart. You're not afraid to challenge me."

"People call me argumentative."

"I'd use the word strong-willed. And spicy." Saint grabs Tabasco sauce and shakes it over his eggs. "I like spice, you know. The hotter the better."

My pussy likes the way he talks, the deep, slow cadence of his voice that sounds like it came from a movie. You can tell he grew up wealthy. He sounds sophisticated, even when he's not trying to be.

"Not many people like spice." I know there's more than one meaning behind his words. He's telling me he likes my personality. It's these unexpected bouts of kindness that throw me off.

"Their loss." Saint shrugs. "What do you like, Jennifer? What do you want?" His question is simple, but there are a million questions underneath it. *Do you want me? Us?* He's probably aware of the bond building between us, the unexpectedly deep connection we've found with each other. Like me, he doesn't know what to make of it.

I swallow hard, looking down at my plate. "I don't know what I want. Not yet."

"That's okay," he says, his voice gentle. "You don't have to know right now. But tell me, Jennifer. What do you see? Five years from now, ten?"

I take a deep breath, letting my mind wander. "I see myself with a degree, a good job. I see myself happy, secure. I see myself... with a family, maybe."

Saint's eyes light up. "A family?"

I nod, a small smile playing on my lips. "Yeah. I always wanted a big family. Brothers, sisters, kids running around, driving me crazy. I want the chaos, the love, the... the family I never had."

He's quiet for a moment, then he says, "I want that too. The big family, the chaos. I want to give my kids the childhood I never had."

I look at him, surprised. "You do?"

He nods, a vulnerability in his eyes that I've never seen before. "Yeah, I do. I want to be a good dad, Jennifer. I want to be present, to love them, to... to be better than my old man."

My heart aches for him, for the pain he hides so well. I reach out, squeezing his hand. "You will be, Saint. You're already so much more than you think."

He turns his hand over, lacing his fingers with mine. "You make me want to be better, Jennifer. You make me want... so much."

The air between us is charged, filled with a simmering tension that's impossible to ignore. I look at him, at his perfect face, his intense eyes, and I feel a longing so deep it hurts. I want him. I want him so badly it scares me.

Someone needs to remind me that the black-haired guy in

front of me is dangerous. Because right now, he feels like the safest person in the world. If I had woken up today in my own apartment, I'd have spent hours listening to Tony's footsteps, waiting for him to go into my mom's room before I scurried to shower. I'd have skipped breakfast and rushed out at the earliest opportunity, eager to be free.

But with Saint, I don't want to go anywhere. I want to be wrapped up in his aura for hours, listening to him talk, watching him eat.

As if reading my thoughts, Saint leans in, his breath hot on my ear. "You're thinking too loud, babygirl."

I shiver, goosebumps breaking out over my skin. "I can't help it," I whisper. "You... you make me crazy."

He chuckles, low and sexy. "The feeling is mutual."

He pulls back, his eyes dropping to my chest. I look down, realizing that my breasts are full, aching with the need to be relieved. I shift uncomfortably, trying to ease the pressure.

Saint's eyes darken, and he reaches out, his thumb brushing over my nipple through the thin fabric of my robe. I gasp, a spark of pleasure shooting straight to my core.

"You're hurting," he murmurs, his voice thick with desire. "Let me help you, Jennifer. Let me take care of you."

I hesitate, then nod, giving in to the need, to the desire. Saint takes my hand, leading me upstairs, his eyes never leaving mine. I follow him, my heart pounding, my body aching. I follow him, knowing that I'm falling, knowing that I'm losing myself to him. And right now, I don't care. Because being with Saint feels right. It feels like home. And I never want it to end.

Saint leads me back into the guest room, shutting the door behind us with a firm click. The room is bathed in soft morning light, but the atmosphere is anything but innocent. The air is thick with anticipation, every breath I take filled with the scent of him, of us.

He turns to me, his eyes hooded, a muscle ticking in his jaw. He looks... hungry. Like a predator about to devour its prey. And I am more than willing to be consumed.

"Take off your robe," he commands, his voice low and authoritative. A shiver runs down my spine, but I obey, letting the soft fabric pool at my feet. I stand before him in nothing but a simple cotton nightgown, my hard nipples poking against the fabric, betraying my arousal.

He steps closer, his breath hot on my face. "You're mine, Jennifer. Your pleasure, your pain, your milk... it's all mine."

I swallow hard, my heart pounding in my chest. "Yes," I whisper. "I'm yours."

He reaches out, his hands cupping my breasts roughly. I gasp, the pressure sending a jolt of pleasure-pain straight to my core. He massages them, his thumbs circling my nipples, drawing a moan from deep within me.

"These tits are perfect," he growls. "So full, so ripe. Made for me."

He pinches my nipples, hard, and I cry out, arching into his touch. Milk leaks from my breasts, soaking through the fabric of my nightgown, leaving dark, wet spots. Saint's eyes darken at the sight, his nostrils flaring like a beast catching the scent of its mate.

"Look at that," he murmurs, his voice thick with desire. "You're dripping for me, babygirl. Such a good little milky slut."

His words should offend me, should make me want to run away. But they don't. They turn me on, make me want more. Make me want him.

He pushes me back onto the bed, his body covering mine. He straddles me, his strong thighs pinning me down, making me feel small, helpless. His.

He grips the neckline of my nightgown, his knuckles brushing against my collarbone. With one swift motion, he tears it open, exposing my bare breasts to his hungry gaze. I gasp, the cool air and his hot eyes making my nipples harden into tight, aching peaks.

"Saint," I whisper, a plea, a prayer. "Please..."

He grins, a dark, wicked smile. "Please what, Jennifer? Please suck your tits? Please drink your milk? Please fuck you like the dirty little slut you are?"

I whimper, my pussy clenching at his filthy words. "Yes," I breathe. "Yes, please."

He chuckles, low and throaty. "Greedy girl. Under that model student act, you're a dirty little whore, aren't you? Needy and desperate for a rough fuck."

I moan. His words vibrate between my legs, drawing moisture from my convulsing pussy.

"Don't worry, baby. I'll give you what you need." He lowers his head, his mouth capturing one of my nipples. He sucks hard, drawing a cry from deep within me. The sensation is intense, a mix of pleasure and pain that has me writhing beneath him. He sucks rhythmically, his cheeks hollowing out, his tongue flicking against my sensitive flesh.

I can feel the milk flowing, my body giving him what he wants, what he demands. He moans around my nipple, the sound vibrating through me, sending sparks of pleasure shooting straight to my clit.

"Fuck, you taste good," he growls, releasing my nipple with a pop. "Like sweet cream. I could drink from you all day."

He moves to my other breast, giving it the same rough, hungry treatment. I arch into him, my hands fisting in his hair, holding him to me. He bites down on my nipple, sending a sharp jolt of pain through me, but the pleasure that follows is intense, overwhelming.

"Saint," I gasp. "Oh god, Saint..."

He releases my nipple, his eyes dark and stormy. "Shut up, Jennifer. Shut up and let me drink."

He latches onto my breast again, sucking hard, drawing out more milk. I can feel it, the tug deep within me, the primal, animalistic need to feed him, to give him everything he demands.

I moan and whimper, my body writhing beneath him. I can feel my pussy, hot and wet, aching for his touch. I reach down, my fingers slipping beneath the waistband of my panties, seeking relief.

Saint releases my nipple, his hand capturing my wrist in a vice-like grip. "What did I tell you about touching what's mine?" he growls. "You're my slave and you have to listen to me. Or I stop."

I nod, my breath coming in short, sharp gasps. "Yes. Yes, I understand."

He releases my wrist, his hand slipping between my legs, cupping my pussy possessively. "Good girl. Now, let's see how wet you are for me."

He pushes my panties aside, his fingers slipping through my folds, teasing my entrance. I'm so wet, so ready for him. He circles my clit, his touch light, teasing. I buck my hips, seeking more, needing more.

"Please, Saint," I beg. "Please touch me. Please fuck me."

He chuckles, his breath hot on my breast. "Such a greedy little slut. Fine, baby. You want my cock? You want me to fuck you like the dirty little whore you are?"

"Yes," I gasp. "Yes, please. Fuck me, Saint. Fuck me hard."

He growls, a primal, animalistic sound. He releases my breast, his body shifting as he undoes his belt, his zipper. I hear the rustle of fabric. And then he's there, his cockhead pressing against my entrance, hot, hard, demanding. He doesn't bother with a condom. And I don't make him. I'm lost in the forbidden heat of the moment, too desperate to feel his cock inside me.

He shoves his massive length into me, filling me completely. I cry out, my body arching, my breasts bouncing. He grips my hips, his fingers digging into my flesh as he fucks me, hard and fast and rough. My back bounces against the mattress. My nerves tingle with pleasure. My body surrenders to his primal, animalistic fucking, a receptacle for his need.

"You look so hot with my cock plunging in and out of your ripe pussy," he growls. "Damn, your cunt is so hot, so tight."

He leans down, capturing my nipple in his mouth again, sucking in time with his thrusts. The sensation is overwhelming, pleasure and pain mixing, merging, becoming one. I can feel my orgasm building, a tight, hot coil deep within me.

"Saint," I gasp. "Oh god, Saint. I'm going to come. I'm going to—"

He releases my nipple, his hand clamping over my mouth, silencing my cries. "Shut up and come, Jennifer. Come on my cock like the good little slut you are."

His words send me over the edge. I come hard, my body convulsing, my pussy clenching around his cock. He groans, thrusting deeper, harder, chasing his own release.

He comes with a roar, his body shuddering, his cock pulsing within me. He collapses on top of me, his breath hot and heavy on my neck.

We lie there for a moment, our bodies twined together, our breaths mingling. And then he pulls back, his eyes meeting mine. There's a softness there, a vulnerability that I've never seen before.

"You're mine, Jennifer," he murmurs. "My personal whore. My milky slave."

And in that moment, I believe him. I believe that I am his, that he is mine. That this, whatever this is, is real.

But even as I bask in the afterglow of our passion, a small, nagging voice whispers in the back of my mind. This is too good to last. Girls like me don't end up with guys like Saint. This is a fairytale, a fantasy.

And like all fantasies, it must come to an end.

NINE

Saint

IT STARTS WITH A TEXT.

SAINT:

I know you like to study but books are overrated. Come get wet instead.

No answer. It's a sunny Saturday but instead of enjoying the weather, Jennifer is studying her ass off, cooped up in her apartment with that asshole of a man her mom is dating. I hate that even that piece of shit gets to spend more time around her than I do. I need to get her out of that house. She doesn't know how to have fun. It's my responsibility to show her, to pull her out of her shell and make her live the life she was meant to live. A life with fun and laughter, not just grades and stress.

So I send another message.

SAINT:

You're not gonna pass your exams if you melt into a fucking puddle. Pool's open. Cold water. Hot company. You know you want it.

Still nothing.

Stubborn little brat. I can imagine her slumped over the textbook, her brown eyes scanning each word like it's the gospel. I know she works hard but she works too damn hard. I've barely seen her all week. Oh, she did the bare minimum, running errands for me, babysitting Easton. And I gave her creamy tits relief in return. But it's not enough to see her every few days. I need her every day. My obsession for Jennifer Garcia is growing into a monster. When she isn't around I miss her. When she is around, I'm scheming of ways to make her fall for me. It should be a game, but it stopped being one long ago. The moment I realized she mattered, the moment I beat my friend for her, it stopped being a game and became a pursuit.

I'm rich so I've never had to chase a woman in my life. That doesn't mean I don't excel at it.

I fire off one more, grinning.

SAINT:

First one here gets a prize. Spoiler: it's my mouth between your legs.

A minute later, my phone buzzes.

JENNIFER:

You're an asshole.

SAINT:

You like assholes. Get moving.

I lounge by the pool in low-slung swim trunks, sunglasses perched on my nose, waiting. My baby bro is not here today. So I decide to do something fun. Jennifer thinks I'm a bully? She's about to find out I'm much more.

The sun beats down on my bare chest as I lounge by the pool, the cold drink in my hand doing little to cool the heat simmering within me. The water shimmers invitingly, but my mind is far from the tranquility of this luxurious haven. It's focused on a problem that needs fixing—Tony.

I dial a number that's etched into my memory, a contact I've relied on for shady work in the past. The line clicks, and a gruff voice answers. "Cross, what do you need?"

Leo, a man with a knack for the underworld and a penchant for getting shit done, is my go-to for situations like this. I don't hesitate to cut to the chase. "I need you to gather dirt on a guy named Tony. Don't know his last name, but I have an address."

There's a pause, the sound of a cigarette being lit. "Alright, what do you want done? Murder, blackmail, simple scare?"

I smirk, dragging a hand through my hair. "Scare the hell out of him. Make sure he understands that he's not welcome back at the house he's living in. There are two women there. They must not find out about any of this. And ensure he breaks up with the woman he's seeing for good. Make him disappear. Far away."

Leo chuckles, a sound that's anything but pleasant. "This job will cost you, Saint."

"Money's not an issue," I retort, my voice hard. "Just get it done."

There's a contemplative silence before Leo speaks again. "You're doing this for a girl, aren't you?"

I hesitate, the question catching me off guard. "What if I am?"

"Then she means a lot to you," Leo says, his tone shifting to something softer, almost amused. "Maybe you're falling in love, Saint."

I scoff, the words setting off alarms in my mind. "It's not love. It's... infatuation. Attraction." Even as I say it, I know it's a lie. There's a gnawing feeling in my gut that tells me it's turning into more.

"Listen, Cross boy," Leo says, his voice serious now. "Nobody goes so far for a girl they're merely attracted to. You're playing with fire here."

I clench my jaw, the truth of his words stinging. Before I can process it, the sound of footsteps catches my attention. I glance up, and my breath hitches. Jennifer is walking toward the pool, clad in a black bikini that leaves little to the imagination. A barely-there, black string bikini that hugs every thick, curvy, fucking *perfect* inch of her body.

Her tits spill over the tiny triangles, round and heavy and begging to be touched. Her waist narrows into those plush hips I dream about, and her thighs—Jesus Christ, her thighs—thick and soft and strong enough to squeeze the life out of me.

Her curves are on full display, her dark skin glistening under the sun. She's a vision, and every primal instinct in me roars to life.

And when she smiles at me, I nearly choke on my own goddamn tongue. I sit up slowly, sliding my sunglasses down to stare at her properly.

She hesitates near the edge of the pool, arms crossing over her chest like she wants to hide.

Not happening.

I curl my finger, gesturing at her to come closer, to sit on the poolside chair beside me.

"I'll talk to you later, Leo," I murmur into the phone, hanging up without waiting for a response.

Jennifer winds her way to me slowly, her tits and thigh flesh bouncing with every step she takes. Flashes with pain and longing grip my cock, turning it hard, making it throb.

"Hey," she says, her voice soft. "Mind if I join you?"

I shake my head, my eyes never leaving her. "You're already late to the party." My voice is rough, filled with a hunger that I can't disguise.

She settles onto a lounge chair beside me, her movements graceful and fluid. I take a moment to admire her—the way her breasts strain against the fabric of her bikini top, the subtle curve of her hips, the long expanse of her legs. She's perfection, and I'm completely, utterly enamored.

"Everything okay?" she asks, her gaze searching mine. There's a concern in her eyes that's genuine, unguarded. It makes my heart clench in a way that's both pleasurable and painful.

I nod, forcing a casual smile. "Yeah, everything's fine."

She narrows her eyes, sensing the lie. "You sure? You looked pretty intense on the phone."

I consider her for a moment, wondering how much to reveal. "Just taking care of some business," I say finally, keeping my tone neutral.

She studies me for a beat longer before shrugging. "Okay." Her gaze drifts to the pool, and she sighs softly. "It's beautiful out here."

I watch her, feeling a possessiveness rise within me. She's mine. Every inch of her, every curve, every secret. And I'll do whatever it takes to keep her safe, to keep her with me. Even if it means getting my hands dirty and paying a fortune.

"You look incredible," I say, my voice low and husky. "Doesn't the sun feel good on your skin? Better than rotting in your room."

My gaze rakes her body and Jennifer pulls back, squirming.

She flushes pink under my gaze. "I look stupid. Like a whale in a swimsuit."

I snort. "You look like sin."

I close the distance between us, making myself comfortable on her lounge chair, leaning into her. The scent of clean soap assaults my nostrils, grounding me in the presence of the beautiful woman whom I can't get out of my mind.

I start at the top.

"You're trying to kill me," I say, my voice rough with need.

My hands slide up, cupping her full, milk-heavy tits. I squeeze gently, feeling the weight, the heat, the way her nipples pebble under my palms.

"Fucking perfect," I murmur, thumb circling her nipple through the fabric. "Big enough to feed me and a whole fucking army. But they're only for me, aren't they?"

She nods, shy but desperate.

I move lower.

My palms skim down her sides, pausing at her soft belly. I kneel in front of her, kissing the curve of her stomach.

"Love this too. Soft, round. Real. Not like those plastic dolls walking around campus."

She gasps quietly, trembling.

I grip her hips, fingers digging into the flesh.

"These hips were made to take me. You know that, don't you? To ride me. To carry babies."

Her breath hitches. I slide my hands down further, to those thick thighs that haunt my every fucking wet dream. I grip one and lift it over my shoulder, forcing her to balance against me.

"Christ, Jennifer. These thighs. Could fuckin' crush me. Could ride my face until I can't breathe, and I'd die happy."

She covers her mouth with her hand, eyes glassy, over-whelmed.

Good.

She should know how fucking beautiful she is. How hard she makes me. How crazy she drives me.

I set her foot back down gently, rising to my full height. She looks up at me, silent, shaking, wide-eyed. I brush my knuckles over her cheek.

"No one ever told you how sexy you are, did they?" I ask, voice low.

She shakes her head. "People often tell me I need to lose weight, though."

I smile, slow and dangerous. "Guess I'll have to spend the rest of today making sure you know what your body does to me."

Her eyes shimmer with something raw. Something I'm not ready to name yet.

I lean in, my lips grazing her ear.

"I wanna see you wet," I whisper. "Wanna see your pretty titties soaked and dripping."

Before she can react, I scoop her up.

She squeals, smacking my chest, but it's half-hearted at best.

"Saint! Don't you dare—"

I walk straight to the pool and jump in, hauling her under with me. The cold water shocks us both, but her body locks around mine like a vice, soft tits pressed against my chest, thighs clamping around my waist.

We surface, gasping and laughing.

I wipe the water from her face and tuck her soaked hair behind her ear.

She's dripping. Shining under the sun.

Beautiful.

Mine.

"See?" I murmur, grinning. "Told you you'd look even better wet."

I grab her face, desperate to taste her mouth. A surge of possessiveness rips through me, a primal need to claim her, to mark her as mine. I lean in, capturing her lips in a searing kiss. She melts into me, her body pressing against mine, her arms wrapping around my neck. The kiss deepens, becoming a fierce, desperate tangle of tongues and teeth, of breath and hunger.

My fingers tease the strings of her bikini. I bite her ear. "I want to see your wet pussy. I want to take you under water until you're coming all over my cock."

It's my private pool, in the backyard of my house, so it's just us here.

She floats against me, weightless in the water, her hands curled into the wet fabric of my swim trunks like she's afraid I'll let go.

I won't.

Not ever.

I brush her hair back from her face, letting my fingers trail down her neck, tracing the delicate curve of her collarbone.

Her breath catches.

The water laps around us, slow and lazy, the summer heat clinging to our skin even here in the cold pool.

"You're beautiful, babygirl," I murmur, my voice rough.

She shakes her head, like she can't believe me, like she doesn't know how badly I mean it.

I slide my hands down her back, pressing her closer until her tits squash against my chest. Her nipples are hard little points against me through the soaked fabric of her bikini.

Fuck, she feels good.

But I don't rush.

I savor.

"You're not just sexy," I say, letting my hands drift lower, resting on the generous swell of her ass. "You're a needy little slut. Your pussy is always drenched for your bully's cock. You deny it, but your body can't deny its needs."

She squirms, trying to pull away, but there's nowhere to go. The pool walls, the heat of my body, the thick tension between us—she's trapped. Exactly where she belongs.

"Saint..." she whispers, breathless.

I smile. "That's right, baby. Say my name."

I hook my arms under her thighs and lift her slightly, letting her straddle me properly. Her bikini bottoms shift, the thin strip of material barely covering her soft pussy. The only thing separating us is a few inches of fabric and whatever scraps of self-control I have left.

And those are fraying fast.

She clings to me instinctively, her face burying in my neck, her thighs tightening around my waist. Every inch of her is slick and hot against me. My cock throbs under the water, so hard it fucking hurts, but I don't move. Not yet.

I want to see if she'll ask for it first.

I slide one hand up her spine, slow and deliberate, until I'm cradling the back of her neck.

"Tell me what you want, Jennifer," I murmur against her temple. "Say it."

She shakes her head.

Prideful little thing.

I chuckle, the sound rumbling through my chest. "You're stubborn even when you're soaking wet and grinding on my cock."

She whimpers softly but still refuses to look me in the eyes.

That won't do.

I lift her higher, forcing her to look down at me.

Her dark eyes are wide and glassy, full of need and confusion and something even deeper she's too scared to name.

I tilt my head. "You think you're in control here?"

She swallows hard.

"You're not," I tell her, my voice dropping to a growl. "I am. And I say we're gonna take our time. Tease a little. Make it hurt."

She shivers, her nails digging into my shoulders.

Good.

Let her feel how much I want her. Let her drown in it.

I lower her slowly, letting the thick ridge of my cock brush right against her soaked pussy through the thin barrier of fabric. She gasps.

I grin.

"Feels good, doesn't it?" I whisper. "Being held. Being teased. Knowing you could come just from rubbing against me if I let you."

Her hips jerk without meaning to. Her eyes flutter closed. I drag my mouth along the shell of her ear, breathing her in.

"But I'm not gonna let you. Not yet."

I shift us toward the shallow end, where I can stand more comfortably with her clinging to me.

Her legs are trembling now. She's so damn close to shattering. Her arms are locked around my neck. I lower her to let her stand on her own in the waist-high water, but I don't let go.

I bracket her between my arms, boxing her in against the pool wall.

Close enough that every breath she takes brushes her chest against me.

Close enough that the heat radiating off her could melt stone.

She looks up at me, defiant and desperate.

I smirk. "When you're ready to beg, babygirl, you let me know."

Before I turn away from her, Jennifer hooks her arm around my elbow.

Her eyes are wide, innocent—Bambi eyes—but the firestorm simmering in her pupils is anything but innocent.

"Saint, please..." she whispers.

I cock my head. "Saint, please what?"

I pinch her chin between my fingers, forcing her to meet my gaze. She resists at first—then gives in.

"There's no shame in wanting things you shouldn't,

Jennifer," I murmur. "I already know you're a needy little whore who likes pain and domination. Nothing you say will shock me. So say it. Ask for what you need."

She swallows, her throat working hard, the good girl inside her warring with the bad. But she's with me—the poster boy for bad decisions. And she gives in.

Her legs lock around my waist. She grips my shoulders, balancing on me, pressing her mouth—*that filthy, perfect mouth*—against my earlobe.

"I want to be ruined," she breathes. "I want you to make me do bad things. Fuck me until I'm seeing stars."

I freeze. That voice—sweet, desperate, broken—slams straight into my cock. Hard. Fucking harder.

She pulls back just enough to look me in the eye, her lips trembling. "Saint, shove your cock inside me and turn my pussy inside out. I need to forget about everything. I've been driving myself so hard. I need you to remind me what pleasure feels like."

My restraint shatters.

My cock jumps in triumph, straining painfully against the wet fabric of my swim trunks.

"Jesus Christ, Jennifer."

She shivers, her body arching into mine. I can feel the heat of her pussy even through the water, the thin barrier of her bikini bottoms. I hook my fingers into the fabric and tug, the material giving way easily. She gasps as I expose her, the cool water rushing against her bare skin.

"Saint," she whispers, a plea and a protest all at once.

"Shh, babygirl," I soothe, even as I grip her hips tightly, positioning her where I want her. "You know you want this. You know you want me to fill you up, to make you feel good."

I reach down, freeing my cock from my swim trunks. It springs out, hard and ready, aching for her. I press the head against her entrance, feeling the heat of her even through the water. She tenses, her body going rigid in anticipation.

"Relax, Jennifer," I command, my voice low and firm. "Let me in. Let me take care of you."

She takes a deep breath, her body relaxing slightly. I push into her, slow and steady, feeling every inch of her tight, hot pussy as it envelopes me. She moans, her head falling back against the pool wall, her eyes fluttering closed.

"Fuck, you feel good," I groan, my hips moving in a steady rhythm, fucking her under the water. The sensation is incredible, the cool water contrasting with the heat of her body, the tight grip of her pussy around my cock.

She wraps her legs around me, her heels digging into my lower back, urging me deeper. I comply, my thrusts becoming harder, faster, the water splashing around us with each movement.

"You're so fucking tight," I growl, my fingers digging into her hips, holding her in place as I fuck her. "So perfect. Made for me."

She moans, her body writhing against mine, her tits bouncing with each thrust. I lean down, capturing one of her nipples in my mouth, sucking hard. She cries out, her pussy clenching around me, the sensation sending a jolt of pleasure straight to my balls.

"That's it, babygirl," I murmur against her skin. "Take it. Take my cock. Let me breed you."

Her eyes fly open, meeting mine, wide and filled with a mix of shock and desire. I hold her gaze, my hips moving faster, my cock thrusting deeper. I want her to feel every inch of me, to know that I'm the one fucking her, the one making her feel this good.

"Breed me," she says the words carefully, like she has realized what she wants for the first time. My babygirl wants a baby in her belly—my baby.

I sink my fingers into her fleshy, baby-bearing hips, kissing her tits as I shove deeper into her cunt, ruining her unprotected walls. Every time my cock scrapes against her soft walls, rapture pours into my blood in thick, inescapable waves. Electric shocks pulse in my veins, numbing my brain, making the sunlight disappear under the darkness of my eyelids.

The coolness of the water only heightens every sensation—the tight clench of her pussy, the frictionless glide of my cock inside her, the way she gasps and pants and clings to me like I'm the only thing keeping her from drowning.

Her thighs grip my hips.

Her tits bounce with every deep, punishing thrust.

I can't stop. She's a glorious sight, eyes closed, begging me, coming undone as my cock plunges in and out of her under water. Gravity and water pressure make it hard to fuck her but I use every bit of my strength to push into her tight channel and wring every last cry from her throat.

"Saint," she gasps, her body tensing, her pussy clenching around me. "I'm... I'm going to come."

I grin, a dark, feral smile. "Good girl. Come for me. Come all over my cock."

She does, her body convulsing, her pussy pulsing around me as her orgasm rips through her. The sight of her, lost in pleasure, is enough to send me over the edge. I thrust into her one last time, pushing against her G-spot, making her cry as her orgasm intensifies.

Her orgasm explodes. Hard.

Her pussy milks me, clenching so violently around my cock that I see fucking stars.

I roar her name into her neck, shooting deep inside her, claiming her in every way that matters. My seed flows out, white streaks floating on the pristine blue water. We're so filthy together, her and I. I love it.

"Oh my god, that was intense." She collapses against me, trembling, whimpering, spent. "I've never done that before. Had sex in a pool."

"Neither have I," I say. "But there's a first time for everything."

She laughs. "I can't believe I made the great Saint Cross do something new."

"You have no idea about the things you make me do," I whisper.

I hold her tight, even as the cool water laps around us, even as the world fades away.

TEN

Jennifer

THE EMAIL HITS my inbox mid-afternoon.

Subject: Tuition Payment Confirmation.

Message: Your account has been paid in full for the academic year. No further action required.

I stare at the screen like it's mocking me.

Paid.

Paid.

I scramble to log into the university portal, fingers trembling. Maybe it's a mistake. A glitch. Some kind of cosmic joke.

But no—the balance shows a fat, beautiful $0.00.

I don't know how long I sit there, frozen, before it clicks.

Saint.

Of course it's Saint.

Who else would casually drop thousands of dollars like it's pocket change? Who else would do something so outrageous, so infuriating, so heartbreakingly kind without even telling me?

Tears sting my eyes, but I blink them back.

I can't cry over this.

I won't.

I MARCH into Saint's townhouse an hour later, still wearing my work uniform from the coffee shop, my hair a mess from the rush.

He's sprawled on the couch, thumbing through his phone like he has *no idea* he's turned my whole world upside down.

I cross my arms. "You paid my tuition."

He doesn't even look up. Just smirks. "You're welcome."

"Saint."

"Gonna need a little more enthusiasm, Garcia. Maybe a parade. A thank-you blowjob at minimum."

I march up to him and grab the phone from his hands. He finally meets my eyes then, lazy and smug, like he's waiting for me to explode.

But I don't.

I can't.

Because underneath the teasing, the cockiness, the stupid smirk—I know why he did it.

And it's breaking me apart inside.

I sit down heavily beside him, the anger draining out of me. "Why?" I whisper.

He shrugs. "I needed a leash on you. This way, you owe me."

I laugh wetly. "Yeah? That it?"

He smirks wider, but there's a flicker of something raw in his eyes. "Pretty much. Leverage. And, you know, your milk's top shelf. Gotta protect my investments."

I punch him lightly in the arm. He catches my wrist and pulls me closer.

"Don't get sappy on me, Garcia," he murmurs, voice low. "You're mine. Gotta take care of what's mine."

The words hit me harder than they should.

I duck my head, biting my lip.

No one's ever taken care of me like this.

Not my mom.

Not anyone.

Just Saint—the boy who once made me cry in a locker room and now... now he's rewriting everything I thought I knew about him.

About myself.

About *us*.

I look at him, this impossible, infuriating, amazing man who has turned my world upside down. He's done something so incredibly generous, and he's acting like it's nothing. Like it's just another day, another act of casual kindness. But it's not. It's everything.

And I want to give him something in return. Something as mind-blowing and unexpected as what he's given me.

I take a deep breath, my heart pounding in my chest. Then, I slide off the couch, kneeling in front of him. His eyes widen in surprise, but he doesn't say a word. He just watches me, his gaze intense and hungry.

I reach for the waistband of his sweatpants, my fingers trembling slightly. I tug them down, revealing his long, hard cock. He's already semi-hard, and the sight of him sends a jolt of desire through me. I lick my lips, anticipation building inside me.

"Jennifer," he growls, his voice rough with need. "What are you doing?"

I look up at him, a small smile playing on my lips. "I'm giving you a thank-you blowjob," I say, my voice steady despite the butterflies in my stomach.

He sucks in a sharp breath, his eyes darkening. "Fuck," he whispers.

I lean in, my breath hot on his skin. I start at the base, my tongue tracing a slow, torturous path up his shaft. He groans, his hands clenching the couch cushions, his body tense with anticipation.

I swirl my tongue around the head, tasting the salty drop of pre-come that's beaded there. He shudders, his hips jerking slightly. I grin, loving the power I have over him, the way I can make him react with just a flick of my tongue.

I take him into my mouth, inch by inch, my lips stretching around his thick cock. He's big, and it's a struggle to take him all the way, but I push through, wanting to give him everything he deserves.

"Fuck, Jennifer," he groans, his hands tangling in my hair. "You look so fucking perfect with my cock in your mouth."

I hum around him, the vibrations making him gasp. I start to move, my head bobbing up and down, my mouth creating a tight, wet seal around his cock. I use my hand to stroke the base, my fingers gripping him firmly.

He starts to thrust, his hips moving in time with my mouth. He's losing control, his body taking over, chasing the pleasure I'm giving him. I love it. I love the way he's falling apart because of me.

"You're a fucking natural, babygirl," he growls, his voice thick with desire. "Such a filthy little mouth. I've turned you into a dirty girl, haven't I?"

I moan around his cock, the sound vibrating through him. I look up at him, my eyes watering slightly, my mouth stuffed full of his cock. He's right. He has turned me into something wild, something filthy and free. And I wouldn't change a thing.

I pick up the pace, my head moving faster, my hand stroking him harder. I can feel him getting close, his body tense, his breath coming in short, panting gasps.

"Fuck, Jennifer," he groans, his fingers tightening in my hair. "I'm gonna come. I'm gonna come in your fucking mouth."

I don't stop. I don't pull away. I keep going, pushing him over the edge, giving him everything I have.

He comes with a roar, his body convulsing, his cock pulsing in my mouth. I swallow every drop, my throat working to keep up with the flood of his release. He tastes salty and sweet, a mix of desire and pleasure that's all him.

I pull back slowly, my lips releasing his cock with a soft pop. I look up at him, my eyes filled with tears, my face flushed with effort. He's breathing hard, his chest rising and falling rapidly, his eyes glazed with satisfaction.

"Fuck, Jennifer," he murmurs, his voice hoarse. "That was... fuck."

I smile, wiping my mouth with the back of my hand. "Did you like it?" I ask, my voice soft.

He laughs, a low, rumbling sound. "Like it? Babygirl, you fucking rocked my world."

I blush, pleasure warming my chest. I did that. I made him feel good. I gave him something he'll never forget.

He pulls me up onto the couch, his arms wrapping around me, holding me close. I snuggle into him, my head resting on his chest, listening to the steady beat of his heart.

"You're amazing, Jennifer," he murmurs, his voice soft. "You're everything I never knew I needed."

I close my eyes, a warmth spreading through me at his words. This is more than just sex, more than just a physical connection. And I'm scared where it may be leading. My heart feels like it'll break if Saint suddenly withdraws his attention, his kindness, his affection from me. I have gotten used to his saucy texts, his ridiculous errands, and his larger-than-life presence.

He makes my days better without even realizing it. He's no longer my bully. He's the man I'm falling for. The man who I cannot help but surrender to.

Our breaths come in unison, filling up the silence in his living room. The place smells amazing and I wish the smell would stick to me so I could relive this experience even when I'm away from him. He lets me sit there, processing, for a long beat before breaking the silence.

"You're coming to a gala with me next week."

I blink. "A gala?"

He nods. "Big deal. Black tie. All the shiny rich assholes will be there."

"And you want me to come... why?"

He grins. "Need a date. And you're my favorite pet project. Gotta show off my new acquisition."

I roll my eyes, but my heart stumbles in my chest.

"Will I be allowed to wear clothes? Or are you planning on parading me around naked for shock value?"

He chuckles. "Tempting. But nah. We'll buy you something classy. Tight, short, backless. Expensive enough that no one questions why a girl like you is on my arm."

His words are cruel.

But his voice—his voice is *soft*.

Like he's already picturing it.

Like he wants everyone to know I'm with him.

And suddenly, the idea doesn't seem so terrifying.

It feels... important.

Permanent.

"Okay," I say, surprising both of us. "I'll come."

He smirks. "Knew you'd say yes. You're addicted to me."

I snort. "In your dreams, Cross."

But deep down, we both know it's not a lie.

I'm already so tangled up in him, I wouldn't know how to leave even if I wanted to.

ELEVEN

Jennifer

I DIDN'T EXPECT Saint to just invite me to a gala and forget about it. But I didn't expect a text from him the next day, asking me to come to boutique so he could buy me some proper clothes. Our eyes met after class but he shrugged it off, hanging out with his friends.

I know it was to prevent people from realizing there's something between us but it stung a little. Me fucking Saint is better left a secret. If the girls on campus find out that he's been sleeping with me for weeks, they'll kill me. I know Saint is just trying to protect me.

But I hate how we can't show our feelings to the world. I wonder if he'll pretend at the gala, too, in front of his posh acquaintances. Pretend that we're nothing more than fuck buddies.

My chest twists with pain at the thought. A dull ache throbs in my lower belly. My ovaries are always excited any time he's around me, ready to jump into action. When he said he'd breed me, I confess I began dreaming of a future together. One where maybe, some day, I could have his kids.

But I know it's naivety. Tony has been missing since last night, and that has given me a lot of time to think. I know he'll turn up again soon but his absence makes me feel safer. Since he ghosted my mom without a word, she has been annoyed. She never talks bad about him but she has been saying how he's acting unreliable. I hope she cuts him off for good. We don't need that parasite in our life.

I make my way to the boutique after my last class for the day.

The boutique is beautiful. Intimidating.

A shrine to silk and sin.

I push open the glass doors and step inside, feeling like a fraud in my worn-out sneakers and faded jeans.

Saint's already there, lounging against the checkout counter, talking to the manager like he's been shopping for high-end dresses his whole life.

When he sees me, his lips curl into a slow, lazy smirk.

"Took you long enough, Garcia."

I cross my arms. "I almost turned around."

He shrugs. "But you didn't."

Because I'm an idiot.

Because I want to see how he looks at me when I dress up like I belong in his world.

The assistant—a stunning blonde with polished nails and a plastic smile—shows me to a private fitting room.

Saint, predictably, follows.

I glare at him. "You're supposed to wait outside."

He leans against the door. "Nah. I'm the sponsor. I get VIP access."

I roll my eyes but grab a dress from the rack anyway.

The first one is midnight blue, silky and scandalous.

I shimmy into it, struggling with the zipper.

"Turn around," I bark.

He chuckles but obliges.

I manage to zip it up and glance in the mirror.

The dress clings to my curves like it was sewn for me.

My breasts are practically popping out. My waist looks tiny. My hips... God. My hips could bring kingdoms to their knees.

My pulse thrums with nerves as I clear my throat.

"Okay."

Saint turns.

And for the first time, his cocky smile slips.

He stares at me like I just punched the air out of his lungs.

"Fuck, Jennifer."

The way he says my name—hoarse, reverent—sends a tremor through me.

I shift awkwardly. "I look ridiculous."

He stalks closer.

Fast.

Predatory.

He towers over me, tilting my chin up with two fingers.

"If you ever say that again," he growls, "I'll bend you over and fuck some sense into you."

My thighs clench automatically.

He drags his eyes down my body, slow and possessive.

"This dress was made for you," he murmurs. "Or maybe you were made for it."

His hand trails down my arm, leaving goosebumps in its wake.

"I want every rich bastard at that gala to look at you and know you're untouchable," he says, voice rough. "Know that you're fucking mine."

The words brand me.

I swallow hard.

Saint reaches behind me, tugging the zipper down a few inches, exposing the curve of my back.

My breathing hitches.

He leans down, his breath hot on my ear.

"Think you can handle that, babygirl?" he murmurs. "Think you can survive everyone wanting what only I get to touch?"

I close my eyes, dizzy.

"Yeah," I whisper. "I can survive it."

Because I'd survive anything for him.

The next is I wear is black, with a plunging neckline that barely covers my nipples. I step out. Saint's nostrils flare.

"Turn around," he says hoarsely.

I spin slowly, feeling the heavy drag of his gaze across my skin.

When I face him again, he's leaning back against the wall, arms crossed, a bulge growing in his jeans.

"You're fucking evil," he mutters.

I grin. "Maybe I've been spending too much time with you."

He makes me try on five more dresses.

Each one sluttier, silkier, more skin-baring than the last.

Each time I step out, his blue eyes darken a shade.

Each time, he praises a different part of me:

My tits. My ass. My thighs.

My *mouth*.

Each filthy word makes me melt a little more inside.

But somewhere between the fifth and sixth dress, the high starts to crash.

Reality creeps in.

I stare at myself in the mirror, at the way the dress hugs my curves, the way my brown skin gleams under the soft lighting.

And I wonder if I'll fit in at all.

If Saint will be laughed at, pitied, whispered about for dragging a charity case to a gala full of CEOs and heiresses.

Maybe I'm just another toy for him.

A project.

A phase.

The thought slices something deep inside me.

I smooth the fabric of the dress nervously and turn to him.

"Saint... maybe you should reconsider," I say, trying to keep my voice steady. "Bringing me, I mean. To the gala."

His face hardens instantly.

Sharp, dangerous.

"Why?"

I shrug, looking away. "Maybe you'll get talked about. Maybe people will think you're slumming it. I just... I don't want to humiliate you."

For a long beat, he says nothing.

Then he crosses the room, crowding into my space, tilting my chin up to force my gaze to his.

His blue eyes burn into mine.

"No one from school's gonna be there," he says roughly. "Even if they were, they wouldn't know what we are."

He smirks, slow and wicked. "Wouldn't *dare* say a word about you."

I swallow.

He drops his hand but doesn't step back.

"Easton'll be there," he adds casually, like it's no big deal.

The knot in my chest loosens slightly.

Easton.

Sweet, perfect Easton.

Knowing he'll be there makes the whole thing feel a little less terrifying.

A little more... possible.

Saint watches me silently for a moment, then tilts his head.

"You ever think about living like this?" he asks. "Wearing shit like this every day. Sleeping in silk sheets. Eating pancakes bigger than your head for breakfast."

I laugh breathlessly. "Wouldn't every girl want that?"

His mouth curves, but there's a mysteriousness to it. A weight behind the question that makes my heart thud hard.

"Maybe," he says, voice low. "Maybe some girls get the chance."

I blink, stunned. Is he implying—?

No.

I squash the thought before it can take root. Saint's not offering me a future.

He's just Saint—dangerous, reckless, untouchable.

And I'm just... me. A girl who should know better. I don't even want the glitz and glamor of his wealthy, privileged world. I just want a chance to...a chance to be with him longer. To hear his witty wisecracks, to feel his skin against mine, to hold him, touch him, kiss him, fuck him, like he belongs to me. Only me.

But when he steps closer and brushes a kiss over my forehead, so soft I barely feel it, a tiny, traitorous part of me dares to hope anyway.

Dares to dream of a future I can never have.

TWELVE

Saint

THE CROSS FAMILY gala is exactly what you'd expect.

Cold. Loud. Expensive.

The chandeliers glitter like diamond stars overhead, raining light onto a sea of tuxedos and gowns worth more than some people's homes. The walls are decked in tasteful gold accents, the music humming with an old money rhythm—violins, champagne flutes clinking, false laughter bouncing off the marble floors.

It smells like money.

And blood.

The predators circling the herd.

I loathe every second of it.

Except for her.

Jennifer stands by the entrance, her red dress clinging to every perfect curve like it was poured onto her skin. The slit up her thigh flashes with every tiny movement, dangerous and mouthwatering.

Her hair is pinned up, loose strands brushing her collarbone. Her makeup is subtle, letting her natural beauty punch you straight in the gut.

She looks like sin wrapped in silk.

And she looks nervous as hell.

Her dark eyes dart around the glittering ballroom, fingers fiddling with the tiny clutch bag I made her carry. She doesn't belong here, and she knows it. Every muscle in her body screams it.

My fists clench at my sides.

Because she belongs with me.

And these fucking vultures don't deserve to breathe the same air she does.

"Saint!"

Easton barrels toward me, dressed in a little tux that makes him look like a baby James Bond. His bowtie is crooked, his hair sticking up despite someone's clear attempts to tame it.

"Hey, buddy," I crouch down, scooping him into a hug.

He wraps his arms around my neck and tugs my hair like he's been missing me for a year instead of a day.

When I glance up, Jennifer is smiling.

Soft. Tender.

It guts me, how beautiful she looks when she forgets to be afraid.

I set Easton down and walk over to her, tugging her close by the waist.

"You're late," I murmur, just loud enough for her to hear.

"You're lucky I showed up at all," she breathes back, voice trembling just a little.

I grin.

"You look fucking perfect."

Her cheeks flush, and I fight the urge to kiss her here and now, in front of every billionaire and senator and socialite in the room.

Of course, that's when *he* arrives.

David Cross.

My father.

He slices through the crowd like a shark in a tailored suit, his silver hair gleaming under the chandeliers, his mouth set in that permanent sneer he's perfected over the years.

His gaze lands on Jennifer.

And freezes.

For one heartbeat, he just stares.

Then he smiles—the kind of smile that would make a lesser man flinch.

"Saint," he says, voice as smooth and cold as a knife sliding between ribs. "A word."

I glance at Jennifer. She tries to look confident, but I can see the way her knuckles whiten on her clutch.

I squeeze her waist once, hard, then follow my father toward the balcony.

The moment we step into the cooler air outside, the mask slips.

He turns on me like a viper.

"What the hell do you think you're doing?" he hisses.

I cock an eyebrow, lazy. "Enjoying my evening."

He laughs without humor. "You brought *her* here. In front of our investors. Our future business partners. You think they won't notice?"

I shrug.

"She's nobody, Saint," he says, voice dripping with disdain. "Some little scholarship case you're fucking between classes.

You think that's what they expect from the next head of Cross Enterprises?"

His words slice deep, but I don't flinch.

I won't give him the satisfaction.

"She's none of their business," I say flatly.

He steps closer, his cologne choking the air between us.

"If you keep this up, you'll embarrass yourself. Embarrass *me*. Maybe I'll have to rethink letting you spend so much time with Easton. Can't have my youngest son influenced by... low-class distractions."

My fists curl so tight my nails bite into my palms.

I don't say what I'm thinking:

That I'd burn Cross Enterprises to the ground before I'd give up either of them.

I just smile coolly. "Thanks for your advice, old man. Always a pleasure."

He sneers again, but before he can unleash more venom, a waiter drifts over, politely offering more champagne.

I slip back inside, leaving my father to stew.

The ballroom feels hotter now. Louder.

I scan the crowd until I find her.

Jennifer.

Standing alone near the far end of the room, looking small and brave and so heartbreakingly beautiful I ache.

Relief floods me.

But then my stomach twists.

Because someone's already talking to her.

Him.

David Cross.

My old man.

I surge forward, heart hammering.

But I can already see it—the way Jennifer stiffens, the way she looks at the floor instead of meeting his gaze.

He's saying something.

Something cruel.

But I can't hear it. Only see the heartbreak in Jennifer's eyes, the fear that paralyzes her expression.

THIRTEEN

Jennifer

SAINT DISAPPEARS onto the balcony with his father, leaving me alone with the swirling glitter and venom of the ballroom. I clutch my tiny clutch bag tighter, wishing I could shrink into the floor.

Everyone here sparkles. Everyone here belongs. Except me.

My skin itches under the weight of their eyes. The ones who bother to look at all. The ones who can already tell I'm an outsider. I breathe through it, reminding myself this is just one night.

Just a stupid, glittering dream I'll wake up from soon enough.

I'm so focused on surviving that I don't notice the man approaching me until he's right in front of me.

David Cross.

Saint's father.

Up close, he's even more terrifying.

All hard edges and cold polish.

The same cutting blue eyes as Saint—only where Saint's burn, his father's freeze.

He stops just inches away, his gaze raking over me like I'm something unpleasant he's trying to scrape off his shoe.

"You shouldn't have come here," he says, voice smooth and venomous.

I blink, stunned.

"Pardon me?"

"You heard me," he says, smiling faintly. "You don't belong here. And you know it."

I stiffen, pride prickling my skin.

"Your son invited me," I say coolly. "Take it up with him."

He chuckles, low and mean. "He would. Saint always did like playing with broken toys."

The words land like a slap.

I straighten my spine, refusing to show it.

"Funny," I say, tilting my head. "He seemed to enjoy being my bully more than my savior."

David's smile sharpens.

"Then you should be grateful he's giving you any attention at all. Girls like you don't usually get noticed unless it's for cleaning rooms or bussing tables."

I flush, my fists clenching at my sides.

"And what kind of girl is that, exactly?" I ask, my voice biting.

He steps closer, lowering his voice so only I can hear.

"A girl with no breeding. No connections. A... colorful background," he says delicately, his gaze flickering over my tan skin like it's a stain. "Parents who probably don't even speak English. No legacy. No future."

I grit my teeth so hard my jaw aches.

"You don't know anything about me," I hiss.

He chuckles again, shaking his head like I'm some cute, stupid thing.

"I know enough," he says. "You think you're special because you have a little sass? A little attitude?"

He looks me up and down with a sneer.

"You're a distraction. Something Saint will grow out of the moment he gets serious about his future."

My stomach twists painfully.

"You think men like him marry girls like you?" David says, voice low and cruel. "Look around. You see any fat scholarship cases clinging to billion-dollar fortunes here?"

I glance at the crowd.

Tall, willowy blondes.

Slender women dripping in diamonds.

Pedigreed perfection.

Nothing like me.

David watches the realization hit me and smiles. It crushes me more than it should. I always knew of the advantages and disadvantages I was born with. But it never mattered to me. I believed I could rise above them. But there are certain places and certain people who will never welcome me, no matter how hard I work or how successful I become.

"My son will associate with women with a name that mean something. With families who own land and banks, not pawn shops and car repair garages. What can you give him? How will you help him in the future?"

He leans in closer.

"Enjoy the sex while it lasts, sweetheart," he says, voice like a dagger slipping between my ribs. "But don't start dreaming. You'll end up exactly where you came from—forgotten. Replaced."

I open my mouth—ready to lash back, ready to tear him apart with words—but the lump in my throat betrays me.

My hands shake.

Tears burn behind my eyes.

I won't cry.

I won't.

Instead, I draw myself up tall, fighting the tremble in my voice.

"You know what?" I say, my lips trembling into a bitter smile. "I'd rather come from nothing than turn into a cold, miserable bastard like you."

His eyes flash—just for a second.

A tiny crack in the perfect mask.

It's the only victory I get.

And it feels hollow.

Because deep down...

Somewhere in the places I don't like to think about...

A part of me believes him.

Believes that this—me, in my red dress, standing in a room full of wolves—was always doomed.

That no matter how Saint looks at me, no matter how he touches me or talks to me when it's just us...

Out here, in this world...I'll never be enough.

I don't know how long I stand there after David Cross walks away.

The champagne bubbles roar in my ears.

The violins sound like sirens.

My throat is raw from holding back the sob clawing to escape.

I can't do this.

I have to leave before I fall apart right here, in front of everyone. Clutching my bag tight against my chest, I slip through the crowd toward the exit, head down, heart hammering. I'm almost at the door when a hand wraps around my wrist.

Firm. Warm. Unyielding.

I jerk to a halt, gasping.

It's Saint.

Of course it's Saint.

He pulls me around, his blue eyes scanning my face, his brow furrowing when he sees the tears streaking my cheeks.

"Jennifer," he says, voice low and rough, "what happened?"

I shake my head, trying to pull free, but he tightens his grip just enough to hold me in place without hurting me.

"Look at me," he commands softly.

I do.

Because I can't not.

His expression darkens, rage simmering just under his skin.

"My father," he growls. "What did he say to you?"

I bite my lip hard, willing myself not to break.

"It doesn't matter," I whisper.

"It matters to me."

He steps closer, shielding me from the curious glances of the crowd with his broad body.

"Jennifer," he says, softer now, gentler, like he's speaking to something fragile. "Whatever he said, it's not true."

The tears spill over, hot and humiliating.

I hate crying.

Especially in front of him.

Especially in this goddamn dress, in this goddamn palace of people who'll never see me as anything but a mistake.

"He's right," I choke out, voice shaking. "I don't belong here."

Saint's jaw ticks.

"You belong with me," he says fiercely.

I let out a bitter laugh, wiping my cheeks with the back of my hand.

"You ever think about what your life would be like without

all this?" I ask, waving vaguely at the crystal chandeliers and velvet and gold.

"Without the family name. Without the money. Without your father's company waiting for you like a shiny fucking trophy?"

He stiffens, just a little.

"You think you could survive without it?" I press, needing to know. Needing something real to hold onto before I fall.

Saint's eyes narrow, but not with anger.

With something heavier.

Something sharper.

"You think too little of me, babygirl," he says quietly.

There's a weight behind his words, a promise he isn't ready to fully give me yet.

But it's enough to rock me.

"You think I don't have other options," he says. "You think I don't have anything without him."

He leans in, so close I can feel the heat of his breath on my lips.

"You're wrong."

I blink up at him, stunned.

There's a ferocity in him I've never seen before.

Not when he fights.

Not when he teases.

Not even when he touches me.

This is different.

This is *real*.

"But if you keep looking at me like I'm gonna break and run," he says, his voice roughening, "you're gonna break *me*."

My heart stutters painfully.

"Saint..." I whisper.

He slides his hand up, cradling my cheek with a tenderness that undoes me completely.

"I'm not him," he says. "I'm not my father. I don't give a fuck about their money, their world, their rules."

His thumb strokes along my cheekbone, wiping away the last stubborn tear.

"You gotta trust me, babygirl."

I hesitate.

Because trust is dangerous.

Trust is stupid.

But when he leans down and presses his mouth to mine—soft, claiming, home—all the fear drains out of me.

I melt into him, my hands fisting his jacket, anchoring myself to the only thing that feels real in this glittering, poisonous world.

Saint kisses me slow, deep, like he has all the time in the universe.

Like he's not letting me go.

Like he never would.

When he pulls back, he rests his forehead against mine.

"Trust me," he repeats, his voice a rough whisper.

And even though every scar inside me screams no...

I nod.

Because it's him.

And for better or worse...

I'm already his.

FOURTEEN

Jennifer

THE LIBRARY SMELLS like old paper, floor polish, and desperation.

Finals week is creeping up, and the place is packed—every table crammed with students hunched over textbooks, laptops glowing in the dim overhead lights, caffeine-fueled anxiety thick in the air.

I find an empty table near the back, away from the worst of the chaos, and pull out my battered laptop. My brain is already foggy, but I force myself to focus.

No distractions tonight.

At least, that's the plan.

I'm halfway through highlighting a particularly dense paragraph about economic theory when a shadow falls over the table.

I don't have to look up to know who it is.

"You're blocking my light," I mutter, scribbling a note in the margin.

Saint chuckles, low and amused.

The sound slides down my spine like warm honey.

"Move over, nerd."

Before I can protest, he dumps his backpack onto the table, drops into the seat across from me, and stretches out his long legs like he owns the place.

Which, in typical Saint fashion, he probably thinks he does.

"You don't even take this class," I hiss, glancing around.

If the librarian catches us whispering, we're both screwed.

He smirks, pulling a thick binder from his bag. "Who said I'm here for the class?"

He flips it open to reveal a blank notebook.

"No notes," I whisper accusingly.

He winks. "Maybe I came for something else."

My cheeks heat, but I duck my head, pretending to read.

I can feel his eyes on me, though—hot, heavy, shameless.

I grit my teeth, refusing to look up.

After a few minutes of stubbornly ignoring him, I sneak a glance.

Saint's leaning back in his chair, twirling a pen between his fingers, watching me like I'm the most fascinating thing in the world.

"What?" I snap under my breath.

He shrugs lazily. "You make a hot nerd, Garcia."

I roll my eyes.

"I'm serious," he says, voice dropping into that dangerous, low purr that always short-circuits my brain. "All focused and frowning like you're gonna save the world with a pie chart."

I snort, unable to stop the smile tugging at my lips.

"Stop distracting me."

"Not my fault you're easily distracted."

"I am not!"

He raises an eyebrow.

Without warning, he nudges my foot under the table.

Then again.

A slow, insistent brush of his sneaker against my ankle.

I stiffen, glaring at him.

He grins, innocent as sin.

"Focus, Jennifer," he teases. "Your future depends on it."

I mutter a curse and bury my face in my laptop.

An hour later, my eyes are burning from staring at the screen.

Saint is somehow still there, flipping through an economics textbook he definitely didn't bring himself.

I lean back in my chair and rub my temples.

"Headache?" he asks, voice softer now.

"A little," I admit. "Just tired."

I don't add that my whole body feels off lately.

Heavy. Sore.

My breasts ache in a way they shouldn't.

I've been flushed and nauseous on and off all week.

Probably stress.

Right?

Saint frowns, studying me like a puzzle he can't quite solve.

"You look flushed," he says, reaching across the table to press the back of his hand to my forehead.

The touch is casual, almost careless.

But it makes my heart thud painfully hard against my ribs.

"I'm fine," I whisper.

He doesn't look convinced.

"You're working too hard," he mutters. "You need a break."

"I need to pass."

"You need to survive," he corrects, his eyes glinting with something fierce and protective.

I swallow hard.

I'm not used to anyone worrying about me.

Especially not like this.

Eventually, the crowd thins out.

The library clock ticks past midnight.

Saint closes his borrowed textbook with a snap and stretches his arms overhead, the movement pulling his t-shirt tight across his chest.

My mouth goes dry.

"You crashing here?" he asks casually. "Or coming back to my place?"

I blink.

"Your place?"

He shrugs. "You're not walking home alone after midnight, Garcia. I'm possessive, not suicidal."

I roll my eyes, but my heart flutters anyway.

"Fine," I grumble.

He smirks, victorious.

WE DON'T EVEN MAKE it to his bed.

I'm so exhausted I collapse onto his massive leather couch, curling into a ball under a throw blanket.

Saint watches me for a minute, something soft and unreadable flickering across his face.

Then he moves around the room, dimming the lights, locking the doors, making sure everything's safe.

When he comes back, he slides onto the couch beside me, tugging me gently into his side.

I don't fight it.

I can't.

I tuck my head against his chest, breathing in the clean, sharp scent of him.

His arms wrap around me like it's the most natural thing in the world.

No teasing.

No dirty jokes.

Just... him. Holding me. Protecting me.

I sigh, my body finally relaxing for the first time all day.

"You're safe," he murmurs against my hair. "Go to sleep."

And for once, I believe him.

FIFTEEN

Saint

THE BAR IS a hole-in-the-wall joint tucked between a pawn shop and a laundromat.

Perfect for conversations that don't need to be overheard.

Leo's already at a corner table when I walk in, a glass of whiskey sweating in his grip, a half-burned cigarette dangling from his mouth even though the sign on the wall clearly says no smoking.

Rules never mattered to men like us.

I slide into the seat across from him, nodding once.

"You're late," Leo grunts, but there's no heat behind it.

"You're old," I shoot back, smirking.

He chuckles, raspy and deep. "Maybe. But I'm still better at my job than any of these new punks."

I believe him.

Leo's a relic of a dirtier, meaner world. And when you need shit done clean, quiet, and permanent, he's the guy you call.

"You got news?" I ask, resting my arms on the scarred table.

He flicks ashes into an empty beer bottle and grins around his cigarette.

"Job's done. Tony's gone."

I relax back into my seat, tension bleeding from my muscles.

"Scared the shit out of him," Leo adds. "Showed him pictures. Reminded him what happens to rats who sniff around places they shouldn't. He won't be coming back. Not unless he's got a death wish."

"You made him break up with Jennifer's mom?" I inquire, to be doubly sure. I don't want dangling threads. Women tend to cling to men unless it's a clean break.

Leo chuckles. "Made him leave her a message. She wasn't picking up. That good enough for you?"

I nod once, pulling out my phone. "Sure, here's your payment."

With a few taps, I wire the money into his offshore account. It's more money than I've spent on anything lately. Then again, you have to pay handsomely for good service in this world.

Leo's phone buzzes on the table.

He glances at it, then nods, pocketing it.

"Always a pleasure, Cross boy," he says.

We sit in silence for a few minutes, nursing our drinks. There's no need for bullshit small talk.

We both know why we're here.

Still, after a while, Leo leans back and smirks at me. There's an oddly philosophical glint in his eyes. Oh shit. That's when I know he's the type to get talkative when he's drunk.

"Gotta say," he drawls, "you're blowing a lotta cash over a girl."

I grunt, sipping my whiskey.

"It's not like that."

"Yeah?" Leo arches an eyebrow. "Funny. I did some digging on her. Had to make sure you weren't tying yourself to a mess."

I narrow my eyes. "You weren't asked to."

He shrugs, unbothered. "Call it professional courtesy."

"And?"

He smirks. "Girl's clean as a goddamn whistle. No boyfriends, no scandals, no skeletons. Works two jobs. Smart as hell, too. Top of her class."

I stare at my glass, something tight curling in my chest. I knew Jennifer was practically perfect but it's nice to have it confirmed. I bet she'd hate to find out someone poked around about her, though. Which is why she'll never know.

"But," Leo continues, "she's not your type."

I snort. "Never had a type."

Leo grins wider, revealing a row of teeth that have seen too many bar fights.

"Could've fooled me. Always figured you'd end up with some cold-blooded heiress. Blonde. Size zero. More ambition than heart."

I think about Jennifer.

Her dark hair.

Her wide, expressive eyes.

Her mouth, so fucking soft.

Her body—thick, warm, lush, real.

Nothing like the girls I was supposed to end up with.

Everything I never knew I needed.

Leo watches me too closely, but he doesn't call me out on the silence. Instead, he leans back, lighting another cigarette.

"You know how I met my old lady?" he says.

I snort. "Not interested in your love life, old man."

But unfortunately, Leo is too drunk to care about what I want. He's determined to tell me old stories and ramble on for as long as he can.

"Was running with a crew back then," he starts. "Dumb, reckless shit. Boosting cars, selling knock-offs. She worked at the town library. Glasses. Cardigans. Always smelling like vanilla and old books."

I chuckle.

"First time I met her, I thought she was boring as hell," Leo says, smiling like he's seeing the memory play out behind his eyes. "But she talked. Jesus, could she talk. About the world. About dreams. About shit I never thought about before."

He exhales smoke toward the stained ceiling.

"She made me feel like I wasn't just some dumb thug. Like maybe I could be more."

I say nothing.

Because the words stick in my throat. Because I know exactly what he means. It's exactly like that with Jennifer. She doesn't talk about celebrities, the latest gossip, or whatever is trending on Instagram. She talks about things that matter. She makes me use my brain. Makes me be intelligent.

Jennifer challenges me. Sees me. Makes me want more than blood and power.

"And when I realized I couldn't live without her," Leo finishes gruffly, "I knocked her up, married her, and never looked back."

I chuckle, shaking my head.

"Romantic," I say dryly.

"Fuck off," Leo mutters, but he's grinning.

He kills his whiskey in one gulp and stands, tossing a few bills on the table even though he knows I'll cover it.

As he slaps a hand on my shoulder, he says, "Don't be stupid, Cross boy. If you find a girl who makes you better, you don't let her go."

Then he leaves, trailing cigarette smoke and regret behind him.

I sit there a long time after he's gone, staring at the door, my whiskey untouched.

Thinking.

Turning shit over in my mind I don't want to look at too closely.

Jennifer.

Soft brown skin, sharp tongue, stubborn pride.

The way she laughs when she forgets to be scared.

The way she melts against me when she lets herself trust.

The way she looks when she's under me—open, bare, mine.

I haven't been using protection.

Neither has she.

Maybe she doesn't care.

Maybe part of her wants it too.

The thought sends a dark, possessive thrill through me.

If she gets pregnant...

If she carries my kid...

There's no way she's walking away from me.

No fucking way.

I swirl the whiskey in my glass, watching the amber liquid catch the light.

Maybe that's a good thing.

Maybe it's the only thing that's ever made sense.

SIXTEEN

Jennifer

THE TEST PAPERS hit the desk with a satisfying *thud*.

The final economics exam.

The last hurdle before freedom.

I stare down at mine, heart pounding, but as soon as I see the big, fat "A" scrawled across the top in red ink, a grin breaks across my face.

I did it.

After everything—work shifts, sleepless nights, endless anxiety—I did it.

"Good girl," a low voice murmurs in my ear.

I jolt, nearly knocking my chair over.

Saint grins lazily from where he leans against my desk, his blue eyes glinting with mischief and something darker.

"You crushed it," he says, tapping the paper with one long finger. "Knew you would."

I roll my eyes, shoving the paper into my bag. "Maybe

because you wouldn't let me breathe without quizzing me on marginal utility curves."

He shrugs, unbothered. "Motivational tactics. You're welcome."

I laugh under my breath, but the warm glow inside me doesn't dim.

It feels good, having someone proud of me.

Even if it's Saint.

Especially if it's Saint.

As we walk out of the classroom into the bright afternoon sun, he falls into step beside me, unusually quiet.

Too quiet.

Which means he's plotting something.

Sure enough, once we're halfway across campus, he says, "You need to unwind."

I shoot him a wary glance. "Define unwind."

He smirks. "My family's lake cabin. Secluded. Private dock. Big bed. Bigger bathtub."

He nudges me with his elbow. "Come with me."

I falter, the invitation catching me off guard.

Just us.

No crowds.

No hiding.

The thought terrifies me almost as much as it thrills me.

"I'm sure you could find someone better to go with," I say, forcing a laugh. "Someone who actually belongs in your world."

He stops walking, grabbing my wrist and pulling me to a halt.

"You want me," he says, his voice dropping into that dangerous low growl that never fails to liquefy my insides. "Or you wouldn't let me fuck you bare all the time."

Heat floods my cheeks.

Saint steps closer, his body crowding mine, his thumb brushing idly along the inside of my wrist.

"You trust me enough to let me come inside you, baby," he murmurs. "Don't act like you don't want more."

I open my mouth, ready to argue—but the words die on my tongue.

Because he's right.

And we both know it.

I cross my arms, lifting my chin defiantly.

"Maybe you're better company than I thought," I admit grudgingly. "Maybe I even... like you."

His eyes gleam with amusement. "You're adorable when you're stubborn."

"But what could you possibly give me, Saint?" I press, heart pounding. "A few good fucks? A couple expensive dresses? I don't belong in your world."

He leans in, so close our noses almost touch.

"I'd give you everything if you let me," he says, voice raw.

The words punch the air from my lungs.

Before I can react, his hands slide up my sides, cupping my breasts possessively through my shirt.

"You're stressed," he murmurs, squeezing just enough to make me whimper. "I can give you relief. All week long."

My entire body flushes hot.

"Saint," I hiss, glancing around.

We're not exactly alone out here.

But he just grins wickedly, thumb brushing over my stiffening nipple.

"You need it," he says, voice like silk and sin. "You *want* it."

I shove him half-heartedly, but my heart is hammering against my ribs, my thighs pressing together helplessly.

God, I do want it.

Want him.

Want the way he makes me feel—wanted, worshipped, real.

Still, I summon enough dignity to mutter, "I'll settle for your friendship."

He laughs, low and dirty.

"Baby," he says, mouth brushing my ear, "you already have more than that."

I shiver.

Because he's right again.

After a long, tense moment where neither of us moves, I exhale shakily.

"Fine," I mutter. "I'll come."

He smirks, victorious.

"You'll be coming a lot," he promises, so filthy my cheeks flame.

He leans in even closer, his breath hot against my ear.

"And don't bother packing clothes," he whispers. "I'm planning to fuck you so much, I need easy access."

I gasp, my entire body going molten, but before I can respond, he saunters off toward the parking lot, whistling innocently.

Leaving me standing there, blushing like an idiot, wondering what the hell I just agreed to.

And why it already feels like the best bad decision of my life.

THE GRAVEL CRUNCHES under the tires as Saint's truck winds down a narrow dirt path, surrounded by towering pines that block out most of the sky.

My heart thuds harder with every turn we take, the city fading further and further away, until it feels like there's nothing left but us and the wild.

When the cabin finally comes into view, my breath catches.

It's gorgeous—two stories of weathered wood and stone, perched right at the edge of a shimmering blue lake. A long dock juts out into the water, bobbing slightly in the breeze. There's a wraparound porch with a swinging bench and a stack of firewood piled neatly near the door.

It's the kind of place you dream about escaping to when everything feels too heavy.

Peaceful. Private.

Perfect.

Saint kills the engine and jumps out of the truck, coming around to my side and yanking the door open before I can even unbuckle.

"Come on, babygirl," he says, grinning wickedly. "Vacation starts now."

I roll my eyes but can't stop the giddy smile pulling at my lips as he hauls me out, tossing me over his shoulder like a caveman.

I squeal, pounding on his back.

"Saint! Put me down!"

He just laughs, carrying me up the porch steps and into the cabin like I weigh nothing.

Inside, it's even more perfect.

The floors are wide, dark wood, gleaming with polish. The living room is all leather couches and thick rugs, a stone fireplace towering to the ceiling. The kitchen gleams with stainless steel and marble counters. A spiral staircase leads up to a lofted bedroom, where I catch a glimpse of a king-sized bed covered in soft white linens.

Saint sets me down, his hands lingering a little too long on my waist.

I step back, trying to gather myself, but the cabin is warm

and cozy and smells like cedar—and Saint is still looking at me like he wants to eat me alive.

I should be nervous.

I should be running.

Instead, I'm smiling.

My heart stutters as I drop my bag by the door.

Saint leaves the cabin for a bit then strolls in behind me, kicking the door shut with his boot.

He drops his bag too and stretches his arms over his head, his t-shirt riding up to reveal a strip of tan, taut abs.

God help me.

He catches me staring and grins.

"Like what you see, Garcia?"

I roll my eyes and turn away, pretending to study the fireplace.

But my body is humming—buzzing with anticipation. It happens so fast I don't even notice at first. I feel a tug, a weird dampness against my chest.

I glance down—

And freeze.

Two dark, wet spots have bloomed over the front of my thin white t-shirt, right over my nipples.

My breasts are leaking again.

Mortified, I cross my arms over my chest, but Saint's already moving.

He's on me in two strides, grabbing my wrists and pulling my arms away, baring me to his hungry gaze.

"Fuck," he groans, voice thick with heat. "You're leaking for me already, babygirl?"

My cheeks flame, and I squirm, trying to tug away.

But Saint's grip is iron.

He presses me back against the nearest wall, pinning me there with the full weight of his body.

"You know what that means, don't you?" he murmurs, his mouth brushing my ear. "Means these tits are aching. Means they need me."

He drops to his knees in front of me, his hands sliding up my ribs, squeezing my breasts roughly through the damp fabric.

I whimper, the pressure sending bolts of pleasure straight to my core.

"Perfect fucking tits," he growls, thumbing my hard nipples shamelessly. "Full. Heavy. Leaking just for me."

I writhe against the wall, the wet heat between my legs growing unbearable.

Without warning, he leans in and licks one soaked nipple through the fabric.

I cry out, my head thudding back against the wood.

The sensation—wet, hot, filthy—is too much.

Too good.

He sucks harder, drawing more milk through the fabric, growling low in his throat like a starving animal.

"Saint—" I pant, grabbing his shoulders.

He shoves the shirt up roughly, baring my breasts, then clamps his mouth over my naked nipple.

Sucking.

Drinking.

Moaning like he's dying for it.

I nearly collapse from the rush of pleasure, from the primal, possessive way he takes from me.

"You're my personal fucking hucow," he snarls against my skin, biting down just enough to make me gasp. "You get that, babygirl?"

I can only nod helplessly, tears stinging my eyes from the intensity.

He slaps my thigh hard, making me jolt.

"Answer me."

"Yes," I choke out. "Yours. I'm yours."

He grins wickedly, his face wet with my milk, his eyes dark with filthy satisfaction.

"Good girl," he murmurs. "Gonna milk you every morning. Gonna suck these sweet tits dry for breakfast."

His hands roam everywhere—squeezing, pinching, worshipping—leaving no inch of me untouched.

I'm panting, trembling, my body arching into him shamelessly.

Needing more.

Needing him.

He stands abruptly, hauling me into his arms like I weigh nothing.

"I told you," he says, carrying me toward the bedroom, "you wouldn't need clothes here."

"And you're gonna prove it, aren't you?" I manage to whisper, half-dazed.

He grins wolfishly, kicking open the bedroom door.

"Every fucking hour, baby," he promises darkly. "Starting now."

THE BEDROOM IS dim and warm, the late afternoon light casting long golden shadows across the wood-paneled walls.

Saint drops me onto the bed like I weigh nothing, and I bounce against the plush, thick comforter, my hair tumbling wild around my face.

He stands at the foot of the bed, staring down at me with dark, predatory eyes.

I feel stripped bare—even though he hasn't removed anything else yet.

"Take it off," he growls.

I push up onto my elbows, heart pounding.

He doesn't move.

Just watches.

So I obey.

My fingers tremble slightly as I peel off my damp T-shirt, baring my breasts fully to his hungry gaze.

His jaw clenches, and he mutters something filthy under his breath.

He takes off his shirt slowly—giving me a show. His body is cut from marble, inked and taut and *dangerous*. His belt follows next, then his jeans, his boxers.

He steps out of them without shame, without hesitation, like he knows exactly the kind of reaction he provokes.

And God help me, my mouth goes dry.

My thighs press together instinctively.

"Saint..." I whisper.

He climbs onto the bed, crawling up my body until he's over me, caging me in with his arms, his weight sinking into the mattress like a promise.

His hand slides up my bare thigh, grazing the curve of my hip.

"You've got no idea what you do to me," he murmurs, brushing his lips against mine.

The kiss starts soft.

Delicate.

Deceptive.

But quickly deepens, his tongue sweeping into my mouth like he owns it, like he owns *me*.

I moan into him, arching my back, pressing my breasts against his chest, desperate for more.

He grinds his hips into me slowly—his cock thick and hard between us—and I gasp at the friction, the heat.

Then he pulls back just enough to look down at me.

"This isn't a quick fuck," he says, voice low and rough. "Not this time."

I blink up at him, heart hammering.

"Then what is it?"

He doesn't answer.

Just cups my face in one big hand and kisses me again—longer, slower, like he's memorizing me.

Like he wants to imprint himself on my soul.

He trails his lips down my throat, over my collarbone, down to my breasts.

He lingers there, sucking gently, licking the droplets of milk that bead at the tips again—but this time it's softer. Worshipful.

And when he lines himself up at my entrance, pressing the head of his cock against me, I shudder all over.

"Saint—"

"Look at me," he growls.

I do.

Our eyes lock.

Then he pushes in.

Slow.

Deep.

Stretching me open until I can barely breathe.

I gasp, clutching his arms, nails digging into his skin.

He doesn't stop.

Doesn't rush.

He fucks me with long, deep strokes, every inch deliberate, dragging over the sensitive places that make me whimper.

"That's it," he mutters. "Take it, babygirl. Let me in. All the way."

And I do.

I *need* to.

He moves like he wants to ruin me gently—like he's not just fucking me, but *claiming* me.

My fingers twist into his hair. My legs wrap around his waist.

We move together, our bodies locking like puzzle pieces, like we were built for this. For *each other*.

Saint buries his face in my neck, groaning into my skin as he thrusts deeper.

"You feel like fucking heaven," he breathes. "So tight. So warm. Like you were made for me."

"Saint—please—"

"I've got you," he whispers. "I've always got you."

His words break something open inside me.

Tears burn behind my eyes.

It's not just sex.

Not anymore.

It's *everything*.

His pace quickens.

My body clenches around him, building and building until I'm shaking beneath him.

"That's it," he groans. "Come for me."

And I do.

With a cry that sounds like his name and nothing else.

My body arches, pulses, *breaks* around him.

He keeps going, fucking me through it until I feel another one climbing right behind the first.

Then he groans, deep and guttural, and spills inside me— hot, thick, *possessive*.

And I love it.

I *love* the way it feels.

I love the way he shudders over me, the way his arms hold me tight like he'll never let go.

And maybe...

Maybe I love *him*.

I lie there afterward, boneless and dazed, his body heavy on mine, his breath hot against my ear.

He doesn't say anything.

Neither do I.

But I feel it between us.

This thing that's growing.

Big. Dangerous. Real.

And terrifyingly unstoppable.

SEVENTEEN

Saint

THE MORNING LIGHT filters through the cabin windows, casting a warm glow over the rustic kitchen. I'm sitting at the table, nursing a cup of coffee, when Jennifer walks in. She's completely naked, her dark hair tumbling over her shoulders, her curves on full display. My breath hitches as I take her in, my cock hardening instantly at the sight of her.

But it's not just her nakedness that has me on edge. It's the milk dripping from her nipples, streaking across her stomach, a stark contrast against her smooth, bronzed skin. Fuck, she looks incredible. Like a fucking goddess.

Her nipples are ripe and swollen. The whiteness of her breastmilk contrasts against the dark brown of her areolae, making her tits like juicy grapes I want to devour.

"Jennifer," I growl, my voice thick with desire. "Come here."

She looks at me, her eyes wide and innocent, but there's a spark of something darker, something needier lurking beneath the surface. She walks over to me, her hips swaying gently, her tits bouncing with each step. Milk leaks onto the floor with every movement. She leaves a trail of white droplets as she walks toward me. Fuck, she looks so hot, gushing milk from her tits like a pregnant woman. Heat fills my cock at the thought of her being pregnant. My balls feel tight imagining her belly swollen and her tits dripping milk over the womb I impregnated.

I push my chair back, spreading my legs. "Sit," I command, patting my lap.

She hesitates for a moment before straddling me, her knees resting on either side of my thighs. I can feel the heat of her pussy against my cock, the thin fabric of my sweatpants doing little to hide my desire.

I reach up, my hands cupping her breasts, my thumbs brushing against her hard, leaking nipples. She gasps, her body arching into my touch. I smirk, loving the way she responds to me, the way her body is so perfectly in tune with mine.

"Look at you," I murmur, my voice low and hungry. "Dripping milk like a good little cow. You're a fucking sight, babygirl."

She blushes, her cheeks reddening, but she doesn't look away. She holds my gaze, her eyes filled with a mix of embarrassment and desire.

I lean in, capturing one of her nipples in my mouth. I suck gently, drawing out a soft moan from deep within her. The taste of her milk is sweet and creamy, like nothing I've ever tasted before. Her breast cream has been getting thicker and more delicious over time. The more I suckle, the more milk her body produces and it's richer, too.

I release her nipple with a pop, licking the remnants of her sweet milk from my lips. Her eyes are glazed, her breath coming in quick pants. I can feel the heat radiating from her pussy, and my cock twitches in response, eager to be inside her. But first, I want to enjoy my breakfast.

I move to her other breast, my hand replacing my mouth on the first, kneading and squeezing, drawing out more milk. She moans, her head falling back, her hips grinding against mine. I can feel her wetness seeping through my sweatpants, and it takes every ounce of my self-control not to thrust up into her right then.

"Saint," she whispers, her voice breathy and desperate. "Please..."

I chuckle, a dark and dominant sound. "Please what, baby-girl? You want me to suck your tits? Drink your milk? You want me to fuck you?"

She nods, her eyes pleading. "Yes. All of it. Please."

I smirk, loving how she begs for me. I squeeze her breast harder, and a stream of milk shoots out, splattering onto her stomach, mixing with the trails already there. I lean down, licking it off her skin, my tongue tracing a hot path up her body.

"You taste so fucking good, Jennifer," I growl, my voice thick with need. "I could do this every morning. Wake up to you, have breakfast right here," I squeeze her breast again, drawing out more milk, "while drinking from your tits."

She shivers, her body responding to my words, her pussy grinding against my cock. I can feel her clit, hard and swollen, rubbing against me, and it sends a jolt of pleasure straight to my balls.

I pull back, my eyes meeting hers. "But first, I want you to taste yourself. I want you to drink your own milk."

Her eyes widen in shock, but there's a spark of curiosity there too. I reach over to the table, grabbing an empty glass. I position it under her breast, my hand squeezing and massaging, drawing out a steady stream of milk. The glass fills slowly, the sound of her milk hitting the glass strangely erotic.

I fill the glass until it's brimming with her creamy milk, the sight of it making my cock throb with anticipation. I set the glass down on the table and turn my attention back to Jennifer. Her cheeks are flushed, her breath coming in quick pants. She's a vision of desire and need, and I can't wait to push her even further.

I grip her hips, lifting her slightly so that I can grind my cock against her clit, the fabric of my sweatpants creating a delicious friction that makes her gasp. Her hands clutch at my shoulders, her nails digging into my skin. I love the little marks she leaves, the evidence of her desire.

"Drink," I command, nodding towards the glass of milk. She hesitates for a moment, her eyes flicking between me and the glass. I reach up, pinching her already hard and drained nipple, making her yelp. "Now, Jennifer. Don't make me ask again."

She leans over, her hand shaking slightly as she picks up the glass. She brings it to her lips, taking a tentative sip. I watch her, my eyes locked onto her mouth as she swallows her own milk. It's fucking erotic, seeing her drink what I've drawn from her body.

"Good girl," I murmur, my voice thick with desire. I slide my hand between her legs, my fingers finding her clit with ease. I rub it gently, teasingly, drawing out a moan from deep within her. Her hips buck against my hand, seeking more friction, more pleasure.

I slide two fingers inside her pussy, feeling the heat and wetness that's all for me. She's so fucking tight, her walls clenching around my fingers as I pump them in and out. Her breath hitches, her body tensing as I bring her closer to the edge.

"Saint," she gasps, her voice barely above a whisper. "I'm... I'm going to come."

"Not yet, babygirl," I growl, my voice firm. "Not until I say so."

I continue to finger her, my thumb rubbing against her clit, my other hand teasing her nipple, rolling it between my fingers.

I continue to finger her, my thumb rubbing against her clit, my other hand teasing her nipple, rolling it between my fingers. She's a writhing, moaning mess in my lap, her body completely at my mercy. I can feel her getting closer, her pussy clenching around my fingers, her breath coming in short, sharp gasps.

"Saint, please," she begs, her voice desperate. "Please let me come."

I smile, a dark and dominant smile. "Come for me, babygirl. Let me see that beautiful face you make when you come for your bully."

She throws her head back, her body convulsing as her orgasm rips through her. Her pussy clenches around my fingers, her juice dripping down my hand. She screams my name, her voice echoing through the cabin. It's the most beautiful sight I've ever seen.

As she comes down from her high, I slow my movements, gently easing her through the aftershocks. She collapses against me, her body limp, her breath ragged. I press a soft kiss to her forehead, a tender gesture that contrasts with the roughness of our play.

"You're so fucking beautiful when you come for me," I murmur, my voice soft.

She looks up at me, her eyes filled with emotion. "You're not my bully anymore, Saint," she says, her voice barely above a whisper. "You're so much more."

Her words hit me like a punch to the gut. I look into her eyes, seeing the truth reflected back at me. She cares for me. She has feelings for me. And fuck, I have feelings for her too.

"I... I have feelings for you too, Jennifer," I confess, my voice rough with emotion. "You're not just some girl I'm fucking with. You're... you're everything."

Her eyes widen, a soft smile spreading across her face. But suddenly, her expression changes. She looks pale, her hand flying to her mouth.

"Saint, I... I don't feel so good," she says, her voice filled with panic.

I freeze, concern replacing the warmth that had been spreading through me. "What's wrong, babygirl?"

I help her off my lap, and she rushes to the bathroom, her hand clamped over her mouth. I follow her, concern etched on my face. She leans over the toilet, her body heaving as she throws up. I kneel beside her, one hand rubbing her back, the other holding her hair out of the way.

"It's okay, babygirl," I soothe. "I've got you."

She retches again, her body shaking with the force of it. I murmur soft words of comfort, my heart aching to see her like this. After a few minutes, she slumps back against me, her face pale and sweaty.

I reach over to flush the toilet, then grab a washcloth from the sink. I wet it with cool water and gently dab her face, wiping away the sweat and the remnants of her illness. She looks up at me, her eyes filled with fear and uncertainty.

"What if... what if I'm pregnant, Saint?" she whispers, her voice barely audible.

I freeze, the washcloth still pressed to her cheek. The thought had crossed my mind, but hearing her say it out loud makes it suddenly very real. I look into her eyes, seeing the fear and the hope warring within them. And in that moment, I know exactly what I want.

"If you are, then I'm happy, Jennifer," I say, my voice firm and sure. "I'm happy to have knocked you up. I'll take care of you and our child. I promise."

Her eyes widen in surprise, a tentative smile playing on her lips. "You... you mean that?"

I nod, a fierce determination rising within me. "I mean it with every fucking fiber of my being. You're mine, Jennifer. And if you're carrying my child, then I'm ready to anything it takes to make sure you and the baby stay with me."

She takes a deep, shaky breath, her eyes filling with tears. "Okay," she whispers. "Okay, let's find out."

I help her to her feet, steadying her as she wobbles slightly. "I'll go get a pregnancy test. You stay here and rest. I'll be back as soon as I can."

EIGHTEEN

Jennifer

I STARE AT THE TEST.

Two pink lines.

It feels surreal.

Like those lines belong to someone else's life.

Someone who isn't shaking.

Someone who isn't trying not to cry.

I blink, trying to force clarity into my vision.

But all I see is the future, crashing toward me faster than I'm ready for.

A soft knock comes at the bathroom door.

"Jennifer?"

Saint's voice is low, cautious. "Talk to me, babygirl."

I open the door.

I don't say anything.

I just hold up the test.

He looks at it.

Then looks at me.

And smiles.

Not the cocky, arrogant smirk I'm used to.

A real smile.

Soft. Fierce. Proud.

He steps forward, cupping my cheeks, his thumbs brushing away tears I didn't even know had fallen.

"You're pregnant," he says quietly, like it's the best news in the world.

I nod, a small, shaky breath escaping me.

"I am."

He leans down and presses his lips to my belly, right over the still-flat skin.

"You're carrying my baby," he murmurs. "Our baby."

The tenderness in his voice undoes me.

"I didn't plan this," I whisper. "It just... happened. But I can't—"

"You're not getting rid of it," he says firmly, standing and pulling me against him.

"I wasn't going to," I whisper. "It feels too precious. Even if it wasn't planned... I've always wanted a family."

His arms tighten around me.

"Then we'll make one," he says. "Together."

I let out a shaky laugh.

"My mom's going to freak," I murmur, burying my face in his chest.

"Then don't tell her yet," he says easily. "Wait until you're ready."

I pull back enough to look at him.

"I have one term left. If I'm only about a month along, I can graduate before the baby comes..."

"You'll start showing," he says, already thinking ahead. "People will talk. Professors. Students."

My stomach tightens.

He tilts my chin up.

"Let them," he growls. "I'll be there. I'll hold your hand when your belly's so round you have to waddle. I'll carry your books. I'll sit next to you in class if I have to."

"Saint—"

"They'll know it was me," he says, his voice dark and proud. "That I knocked you up. Stuffed my brat inside you. And I won't be ashamed of that. I *want* them to know."

My cheeks burn, but I can't help the way my heart soars.

Still, I shake my head gently. "Not yet. Please. I want to keep it quiet until I start showing."

He nods after a beat.

"Okay. But when it's time, I'm standing beside you. No hiding. No shame."

His fingers slide down to rest against my stomach.

"I want the world to know you're mine."

I rest my hand over his.

"You want me to move in with you now, don't you?"

He nods. "It's safer. Easier."

"I don't know." I hesitate. "I need time to think about it. And I don't want your dad finding out until I'm showing."

Saint's jaw tightens.

"Don't worry about him. He needs me more than I need him."

I raise an eyebrow.

He exhales, stepping back slightly and rubbing a hand over his jaw.

"My mom came from money. Her family set up a trust for me before she died. The kind of trust even my old man can't touch."

I blink, surprised.

"So... you'd still be okay if he cuts you off?"

Saint looks at me, his expression hard and certain.

"I'd still have enough to take care of you. Of the baby. Of everything. Money will never be a problem, Jennifer."

My shoulders sag with relief.

"God," I whisper. "You've really... thought about all this."

He steps closer, sliding a hand over my belly again.

"I've been preparing for this since the first time I came inside you," he says. "I wanted this. Wanted to breed you. Fill you up. Start a family with you."

The words steal my breath.

"You're going to be the perfect mom to my kids."

I laugh softly, heart clenching at the way he says *kids.*

"Kids? Plural?"

He grins wickedly, leaning in to kiss my jaw.

"Babygirl," he murmurs, lips brushing my skin, "once you pop out this one, I'm breeding you again. And again. I can't resist this body. I want it round and full of my babies for the rest of my fucking life."

I tremble at his words.

At the fierce love behind them.

He pulls back just enough to look me in the eyes.

"You're everything to me," he says. "And now you're giving me everything I've ever wanted."

I cup his face, my eyes stinging.

"I'm scared," I admit.

"So am I," he whispers. "But we've got this. You've got me."

He leans down and kisses me—slow, deep, filled with promise.

And in that moment, I believe him.

THE MORNING LIGHT filters through the cabin windows, casting a soft glow over the room. I stir awake, the warmth of Saint's body pressed against mine, his arm draped protectively around my belly. His hand cradles the slight swell where our baby grows, a silent promise of his commitment and care.

I turn my head slightly, gazing at his sleeping face. He looks so peaceful, so content. A small smile plays on my lips as I whisper to him, even though he's fast asleep. "I'd never want to do this with anyone but you, Saint."

My mind races with a whirlwind of thoughts. Saint is reliable, wealthy, and from what I've seen with Easton, he's going to be an amazing dad. Our child couldn't ask for a better father. But there's a gnawing anxiety in the pit of my stomach. He's out of my league—the rich, handsome, popular guy who could have anyone he wants. And yet, here he is, by my side, choosing me.

I caress my belly gently, a sense of wonder and joy spreading through me. I never imagined I'd get knocked up when I started hanging out with him. It wasn't part of the plan, but now that it's happening, I can't help but smile. I'm happy to have Saint and this baby in my life. I know that for sure.

I watch him sleep, the rise and fall of his chest, the gentle flutter of his eyelashes. He's so beautiful, so strong, and yet, there's a vulnerability in his sleep that tugs at my heart. He's been through so much, and he's still willing to take on this new challenge with me.

The cabin is quiet, save for the soft rustling of leaves outside and the distant chirping of birds. It's our last peaceful day here before we head back to reality. I want to savor every moment, to soak in the tranquility and the connection we share.

I rest my head on his chest, feeling the steady beat of his heart. It's a comforting rhythm, a reminder of his strength and stability. With each breath he takes, I feel a sense of peace wash over me. This is where I feel loved, feel safe and protected.

I wish I could stay here in the cabin with Saint until our baby comes along but reality is waiting for me.

I'll have to sign up for summer school and take summer classes so I can graduate even earlier and have enough time to prepare to give birth. But I'm not scared.

Because deep in my soul, I know this is everything I wanted. A gorgeous man who makes my heart flutter and his baby in my belly.

NINETEEN

Jennifer

PREGNANCY IS EXHAUSTING.

People don't talk enough about that part.

It's not the romantic, glowing, pickles-and-ice-cream montage I thought it would be.

It's nausea that creeps in before dawn and refuses to leave.

It's being bone-tired in a way coffee can't fix.

It's crying at a dog food commercial because the golden retriever looked lonely.

And yet...

Somehow, it's also the safest I've ever felt.

Because Saint is everywhere.

He's in the kitchen every morning making me scrambled eggs—no smell, just salt and pepper, the way I can stomach them.

He's beside me in class, taking notes for both of us while I nap through half the lecture with my head on his shoulder. He tells me I just need to sleep and attend lectures—he'll do the rest. He paid my tuition, too, and I was touched by the gesture. He really is a responsible father and an even better boyfriend who devotes all his time and energy to taking care of me.

He's on campus every single day, whispering things like *"You're growing our baby, babygirl. I'll do the rest."* into my ear between classes.

He's... consistent.

And that's the scariest part of all.

I signed up for summer classes to graduate early. I figured it was the smart thing to do—finish my degree before I'm too big to sit comfortably in the too-small desks in Room 112.

What I didn't expect was for Saint to sign up with me.

He leaned in during registration and whispered, "Figure I should graduate early too. Free up more time to spoil you and our spawn."

He says things like that—casual, cocky, infuriatingly sweet.

Sometimes I want to punch him in the mouth.

Other times, I want to kiss him until I forget how afraid I am.

"DID YOU TAKE YOUR VITAMIN?" he asks one afternoon, sliding a Tupperware of chopped mango across the table to me.

I pop the gummy in my mouth and nod, chewing.

"Good," he murmurs, brushing a kiss to my temple like it's the most normal thing in the world.

He feeds me fruit, rubs my back, and reads me excerpts from *What to Expect When You're Expecting* in his deep, sarcastic voice that somehow makes even pelvic floor exercises sound erotic.

I should be suspicious of how easy he makes it all seem.

But I'm too tired.

Too... happy.

We spend every evening at his townhouse now. It's where I feel the coziest and most protected. We're all alone, with nobody to pop our bubble of love and intimacy. No prying eyes watching us. No judgmental words destroying the safe haven we're created for our child and ourselves.

I tell my mom I'm doing "group study," which isn't even technically a lie. Sometimes we do read.

Okay, we read baby books.

Mostly while kissing.

Or while Saint is lying on the couch with his hand on my belly like he's protecting it from the world.

"Feel anything yet?" he asks one night, nudging my bump with his knuckle.

"Just gas," I mumble, shoving a pillow under my back.

He laughs, low and rough.

"I'll take it. Our baby's already got fight."

TWO MONTHS LATER...

WE'RE CURLED up on the oversized sectional at Saint's townhouse, his head on my shoulder, my legs draped over his lap. A bowl of half-melted ice cream rests on my swollen stomach, forgotten.

On the TV, some nature documentary plays in the background, a narrator calmly discussing the mating rituals of penguins. It's peaceful. Domestic. Almost laughably normal.

And then I say it.

"I think my mom's happier now."

Saint hums lazily beside me. "Yeah?"

I nod. "Tony ghosted her."

His fingers still against my thigh.

I feel it. The subtle shift in energy.

"Really?" he says casually. Too casually.

"Yeah," I reply slowly, narrowing my eyes. "He just disappeared one day. No warning. No texts. Nothing. One second he was there, and the next... gone."

Saint adjusts his position, reaching for the remote to lower the volume. "Hmm."

My suspicion spikes.

"Hmm?" I repeat, sitting up slightly. "That's all you've got?"

"What else should I say?" he deflects, not meeting my eyes.

I narrow mine. "Saint..."

He groans, tossing his head back against the couch. "Don't give me that look, Garcia."

I fold my arms over my belly, my voice low. "What did you do?"

His jaw tightens.

"What. Did. You. Do?"

He exhales slowly, scrubbing a hand down his face.

"I made sure he wouldn't be a problem."

The words land like a thunderclap.

My heart races.

"You *what?*"

"I didn't touch him," he says quickly. "Didn't lay a finger on him."

"Then how—"

"I made a call. Had someone pay him a visit. Scared him off."

I stare at him.

"You ran him out of town."

Saint finally looks at me, his eyes blazing.

"I didn't want a creep like that anywhere near you. And definitely not around our kid."

The possessiveness in his voice is sharp. Clear. Unapologetic.

My breath catches.

"You're already being overprotective," I murmur. "Like... full-on Dad mode."

He lifts a brow, leaning forward. "What did you expect me to be?"

"I don't know," I whisper. "I didn't expect any of this."

His fingers brush over my knee.

"You think I'd let anyone threaten my family? You think I'd sit back while you were living in the same apartment as some asshole who looks at you like you're prey?"

I look at him, really look at him. The hard jaw, the clenched fists, the fierce eyes.

He would burn down the world. I believe that now.

And I love him for it.

So I say it.

Quietly. Clearly.

"I love you."

His whole body stills.

He blinks. Then slowly, a crooked smile tugs at his lips.

"Yeah?" he murmurs, a softness in his voice I've never heard before.

"I do," I whisper. "For the way you take care of me. The way you look at me like I'm your whole world. For everything."

He leans in and kisses me, slow and deep, his hand cupping the side of my face.

When he pulls back, his voice is raw.

"I was scared you'd never look past the asshole exterior.

Never see anything but the rich bad boy who gave you hell that first semester."

I shake my head, smiling. "I'm a smart girl. I can spot a good thing when I see one."

He chuckles, his eyes twinkling. "Damn right you can."

We settle back into the couch, his hand stroking slow, lazy circles over my belly.

"So," I murmur, "what do you think Professor Lyle's going to rant about tomorrow?"

"Probably how none of us understand marginal utility and we're all going to fail in the real world," he grumbles. "Same as every week."

I laugh softly. "I like sitting next to you in class."

"I like *being* in class," he says, surprising me.

"You do?"

"I used to hate it. But now..." he shrugs. "I get to be with you. Watch you scribble angry notes and pretend you're not turned on when I whisper filthy things in your ear during lectures."

My cheeks flush, and I nudge his shoulder. "You're the worst."

"Maybe," he says, then leans in, dropping a kiss just under my ear. "But I'm your worst."

I smile, my heart full.

There's a pause. A beat of quiet.

Then he adds, almost too softly, "I started bullying you because I liked you."

I blink.

"You *what*?"

"I didn't know how else to get your attention. You were so serious. So untouchable. I figured if I annoyed you enough, you'd notice me. Maybe even like me back."

"You were such an asshole."

"Yeah," he agrees. "But it worked, didn't it?"

My laughter fills the room.

And then he lays his head on my lap again, pressing his ear to my belly.

"You think I'll hear it this time?" he whispers.

"No," I murmur, brushing his hair back. "But I think they hear you."

He closes his eyes, his palm splayed protectively over our child.

And I memorize this moment.

Because it feels like forever.

Even if I'm scared it won't last.

TWENTY

Saint

THREE MONTHS LATER...

TWO PINK LINES.

That's all it took to change everything.

Now we're halfway through the third trimester, and Jennifer is showing.

Not "might be bloated" showing.

I'm talking round belly, swollen tits, waddling slightly when she walks showing.

And the entire campus has taken notice.

I keep my hand on her belly almost constantly now—half because I like feeling the little kicks, half because I want everyone to see exactly what's mine.

Especially the assholes whispering behind their Starbucks cups.

"Did you see her stomach? Jesus, Saint must've really slummed it."

"I guess she was easy after all. He always did like the messed-up ones."

"Think he'll stick around once the kid's out?"

They think I don't hear them.

They're wrong.

I turn to the latest offender—Liam Hayes, legacy frat boy with a trust fund and a jawline that could cut glass but no personality to match—and smirk.

"She's carrying my kid," I say loud enough for half the quad to hear. "What have you contributed to the gene pool, Hayes? A failed econ midterm and a trail of broken condoms?"

The laughter stings him. Good.

I slide my arm tighter around Jennifer, tucking her against my side.

She's pretending not to hear them, but her grip on her books has gone white-knuckle.

I lean down, murmuring just loud enough for her ears alone.

"They'll eat their words when they see you glowing in white, babygirl."

She blinks up at me, startled.

I don't elaborate.

I'm working on it.

We've got two months left until graduation.

Two months until we're out of here.

And I'm determined to make sure we finish strong.

We need these degrees. Not because I care about the piece of paper, but because Jennifer deserves the security. She deserves options. So do I.

When my father cuts me off—and I know it's a *when*, not an *if*—I need something to fall back on.

Something I've earned on my own.

Not just for me.

For her.

For our baby.

For the life I'm building outside my father's shadow.

LATER THAT EVENING, after walking Jennifer back to my townhouse and tucking her into the couch with two pillows and a half gallon of chocolate milk, I step out onto the porch and dial Leo.

He picks up on the second ring.

"Tell me you're not calling about another guy who needs a 'talking-to.'"

"Not this time," I say, watching the sunset over the lake. "I need a ring. I have to propose to my girlfriend."

There's silence on the line. Then a bark of laughter.

"You're using a thug to buy an engagement ring now?"

"I can't use my card," I mutter. "My dad monitors everything. If he sees a charge at Tiffany's or some fancy-ass jeweler, he'll know."

"So you want me to do your wedding shopping. Jesus."

"Just something real. No fake stones. Classic. She's not flashy. A solitaire will do."

Another pause. Then: "Damn, Cross. Never thought I'd see the day. You're whipped."

"Maybe."

"But it's a good look on you."

I hear him lighting a cigarette.

"You ready?" he asks. "To be a dad?"

I think of the way Jennifer rests her hands on her belly now, absentmindedly protective. I think of the baby clothes she's started researching, the quiet way she whispered *'I love you'* last week like it scared her to say it out loud.

"As ready as I'll ever be."

Leo exhales a stream of smoke into the receiver. "You've got a good thing, kid. Don't let anyone fuck with it."

"I don't plan to."

Back inside, Jennifer's curled on the couch, one of my old sweatshirts stretched over her belly. She's reading an article on her phone, but I know she's been hearing things on campus too.

People talk.

They always do.

She pretends not to care.

But sometimes...

Sometimes I see it.

The flash of insecurity when someone whispers too close.

The way her hand instinctively covers her belly when a girl from our class gives her a judgmental once-over.

She hasn't said it aloud.

But I know what she's thinking.

What if he leaves once the baby's born?

What if this is temporary?

The truth is... there's no reason for me to stay.

No contract. No leash.

No family expectation pushing me to stick with the middle-class Hispanic girl I knocked up.

But I'm not leaving.

I'm marrying her.

Soon.

And when I do, I'll make sure she never doubts again.

She looks up as I sit down next to her.

"My mom's okay with it," she says softly.

"With the baby?"

"Yeah. I didn't tell her who the father is. She didn't ask.

But... she's being supportive. Weirdly. And she hasn't mentioned Tony."

I nod, something warm settling in my chest.

"Then our baby's got at least one grandparent who'll be around."

She smiles, tired but real. "Yeah."

I slide my hand over her belly, fingers splaying protectively.

"And me," I say. "They've got me."

She leans into my side, her head on my shoulder.

"Don't say anything," I murmur, "but you've made this place kind of tolerable."

"College?"

I nod. "I used to hate it. But now... you're here. So it's better."

She glances up. "You're just saying that because you like watching me in leggings during lectures."

"That too," I smirk. Then I go quiet for a moment. "You know I started bullying you because I liked you, right?"

She raises an eyebrow.

"Seriously. I didn't know how to flirt. You were so... untouchable. Smart. Confident. I wanted you to notice me. And I figured being an ass was better than being invisible."

She shakes her head, laughing softly. "You really are something else."

I kiss her forehead.

And quietly, I think about the ring Leo's going to find for me. About the proposal. I'm going to wow Jennifer, make her feel gorgeous and special, reassure her about the future. I'll make it the most special day of her life. It'll be grand yet intimate.

For the first time in my life, I'm not afraid of what comes next.

Because I know exactly what I want.

And she's lying right here beside me.

Jennifer shifts beside me on the couch, her baby bump pressing against my side. She looks up at me with those dark, uncertain eyes, and I can see the questions swirling in them. But I don't want her to doubt, not even for a second. I want her to feel desired, to know that she's everything to me.

I lean in, capturing her lips in a fierce, hungry kiss. She melts into me, her body soft and pliant. I slide my hand up her thigh, feeling the warmth of her skin through her leggings. She gasps into my mouth as my fingers find the heat between her legs, teasing her through the fabric.

"Saint," she whispers against my lips, her voice breathy and needy.

"Shh, babygirl," I murmur, trailing kisses down her neck. "I've got you. I'm going to make you feel so good."

I pull her onto my lap, her belly pressing against my abs. I can feel the life inside her, the life we created together, and it turns me on more than anything else. I grip her hips, my fingers digging into her soft flesh as I grind against her.

"You're so fucking sexy, Jennifer," I growl, my lips trailing down to her collarbone. "Your body is perfect, every curve, every inch. You're carrying my baby, and it makes you even more desirable."

She shivers, her eyes fluttering closed as my hands slide up to cup her breasts. They're fuller now, swollen with the promise of milk. I squeeze them gently, feeling their weight, their softness.

"These tits," I murmur, my voice thick with desire. "They're going to fill with milk again, all because of the kid I gave you. You're fucking perfect, babygirl. Made for me."

I capture one of her nipples in my mouth, sucking gently. She moans, her head falling back, her body arching into mine. I suck harder, drawing out a gasp from deep within her. I can feel her responding to me, her body coming alive under my touch.

"Saint," she gasps, her fingers tangling in my hair, holding me to her as if she's afraid I'll stop. But I have no intention of stopping. I'm addicted to her, to her taste, to her scent, to the way she responds to me.

I move to her other breast, giving it the same attention, sucking and teasing her nipple until she's writhing in my lap. Her breath comes in short, sharp gasps, and I can feel the heat radiating from her pussy, even through her leggings.

"You're so fucking wet for me, aren't you, babygirl?" I murmur against her skin, my hands sliding down to grip her ass, pulling her closer to me. "You're dripping, ready for my cock."

She nods, her eyes glazed with desire. "Yes," she whispers. "I'm always ready for you, Saint."

I growl, a primal sound that comes from deep within me. "Good girl. Now stand up and take off those leggings. I want to see you."

She hesitates for a moment, a flash of insecurity crossing her face. But I don't want her to feel insecure, not with me. I want her to know that she's the most beautiful thing I've ever seen.

"Jennifer," I say, my voice firm. "I'm going to fuck you hard so I can watch that sexy pregnant stomach bouncing. Now stand up and show me that beautiful body of yours."

She takes a deep breath and stands up, her hands trembling slightly as she peels off her leggings. She stands before me, naked and vulnerable, her baby bump proud and round, her breasts full and heavy. She's a goddess, and she's all mine.

I stand up, towering over her, and grip her chin, tilting her head up to look at me. "You're fucking perfect," I say, my voice rough with emotion. "I want to paw those massive mommy tits and stuff another baby up your cunt. I want your belly even bigger with twins."

I drop to my knees in front of her, my hands sliding up her thighs, spreading her legs wider. Her pussy is right there, glistening and ready for me. I lean in, inhaling her scent, the smell of her arousal filling my senses. She's so fucking wet, so ready for me, and it drives me wild.

"You're dripping for me, babygirl," I growl, my voice thick with desire. "You want my cock inside you, don't you?"

She nods, her breath coming in quick pants. "Since my morning sickness went away, I've been craving sex but I was too scared to ask."

I stand up, towering over her once again. I can see the desire in her eyes, the need that matches my own. I unzip my pants, freeing my hard cock, and she watches me with hungry eyes.

"Get on the couch," I command, my voice firm. "On your hands and knees."

She does as I say, positioning herself on the couch, her ass in the air, her pussy glistening and ready for me. I step up behind her, my hands gripping her hips, my cock poised at her entrance.

"Fuck, you look so good like this," I murmur, my voice filled with lust. "Your ass, your hips, your curves. I love watching your swollen womb bouncing with my thrusts."

I thrust into her, filling her completely. She cries out, her body arching as I begin to move, my hips slamming against hers, my cock driving deep inside her. Her baby bump bounces with each thrust, a visual reminder of the life we created together. It's so fucking sexy, so primal and raw.

"Saint," she cries out, her voice filled with pleasure. "Oh God, Saint, you feel so good."

I can feel the heat of her pussy, the tight grip of her walls around my cock. I increase my pace, my thrusts becoming harder, faster, my hands gripping her hips tightly. Her breasts jiggle with each movement, her body bouncing against mine.

It's the best feeling in the world, thrusting inside the pussy I bred. Feeling the cunt I stuffed and impregnated. My cock twitches the closer I get to her cervix. When I bump against her womb's entrance, Jennifer groans.

Heat pours through my system, incinerating any self-control. I grab her hips, cradling her swollen stomach as I push harder, deeper into her pliant pussy. Her walls choke my cock, so needy and desperate. Her pregnant body demands my release, making sparks climb up my spine, squeezing it until my brain's blanking out from the intense pleasure.

I grip her hips tighter, my fingers digging into her soft flesh as I pound into her from behind. Her pregnant belly swings gently with each thrust, a visual reminder of the life we created together. It's fucking sexy, seeing her like this, knowing I did this to her.

"Fuck, Jennifer," I growl, my voice rough with lust. "Your pussy is so fucking tight. It's so needy for a cock, even though you're round and swollen with the consequences of taking my cock in your bare pussy."

She moans, her body trembling as I slam into her again and again. I can see the sweat glistening on her skin, the flush of pleasure spreading across her cheeks. She's so fucking beautiful, so sexy, and she's all mine.

"You like that, babygirl?" I grunt, my hips moving faster, my cock driving deeper into her. "You like being fucked like this, with my baby inside you?"

She nods, her breath coming in quick gasps. "Yes, Saint. I love it. I love feeling you inside me."

I reach around, my hand finding her swollen clit. I rub it roughly, drawing out a cry of pleasure from deep within her.

Her pussy clenches around my cock, her body responding to my touch.

"That's it, babygirl," I murmur, my voice thick with desire. "Come for me. Come all over my cock. Show me how much you love being bred by me."

She throws her head back, her body convulsing as her orgasm rips through her. Her pussy pulses around my cock, her juices coating my shaft. I can feel the heat of her release, the intensity of her pleasure.

"Fuck, yes," I groan, my hips moving faster, my cock thrusting deeper.

I can feel my own orgasm building, the pressure in my balls becoming almost unbearable. I grip her hips tighter, my fingers leaving marks on her skin as I slam into her one last time, my cock pulsing as I spill my seed deep inside her.

"Fuck, yes," I groan, my body shaking with the force of my release. "I love breeding you, Jennifer. I love filling you with cum, knowing that I'm the one who put this baby inside you."

She collapses onto the couch, her body trembling with the aftershocks of her orgasm. I pull out of her, my cock still hard, still eager for more. I turn her over, my eyes raking over her body, taking in every curve, every inch of her.

"You're so fucking sexy, Jennifer," I say, my voice filled with lust. "Your body is perfect, so ripe and ready. You're a fucking goddess, and you're all mine."

I lean down, capturing her lips in a fierce, hungry kiss. She melts into me, her body soft and pliant, her arms wrapping around my neck. I can taste the salt of her tears, the sweetness of her pleasure.

"I love you, Saint," she whispers against my lips. "I love you so much."

Her words send a surge of emotion through me, a feeling of

possessiveness and protectiveness that's almost overwhelming. I pull back, my eyes meeting hers.

"I love you too, Jennifer," I say, my voice firm. "You're mine, and I'm yours. And I'll take care of you, always."

I slide my hand over her belly, feeling the life inside her, the life we created together. It's a reminder of our connection, of the bond that ties us together. I lean down, pressing a soft kiss to her stomach.

"And I'll take care of our baby," I murmur. "I'll be the best fucking dad I can be. I promise."

She smiles up at me, her eyes filled with love and trust. In that moment, I know that I'll do everything in my power to protect her, to cherish her, to make her happy. She's my world, my life, my everything. And I'll never let her go.

TWENTY-ONE

Jennifer

THE EARLY MORNING sun casts a harsh glare on the worn-out sidewalk as I step out of my apartment, my arms hugging my textbooks to my chest. My belly, round and prominent, leads the way, a constant reminder of the life growing inside me. I'm six months pregnant, and even though I'm showing, I'm determined to finish this semester. I can do this. I have to.

As I turn to lock the door, a shiver runs down my spine. I feel eyes on me, a heavy, unwelcome gaze. I glance up, my heart pounding in my chest, and there he is—Mr. David Cross, Saint's father, standing a few feet away, his arms crossed, his eyes cold and calculating. He's been waiting for me.

My breath catches in my throat, and I instinctively cradle my belly protectively. Nervousness and anxiety surge through me, making my palms sweat and my heart race. I knew this moment would come eventually, but I didn't expect it to be today, not like this.

"Jennifer," he says, his voice devoid of warmth. "We need to talk."

I swallow hard, trying to steady my voice. "Mr. Cross, I'm on my way to class. Can this wait?"

He scowls, his eyes dropping to my stomach, lingering on the evidence of my pregnancy. "I think you know why I'm here. The rumors have reached me, and I can see they're true."

I take a deep breath, trying to calm my racing heart. "I don't know what you've heard, but—"

"Don't play dumb with me, girl," he snaps, his voice like a whip. "You're pregnant with my son's child. You've trapped him, and now you're ruining his future."

His words hit me like a punch to the gut. I stagger back slightly, my arms tightening around my belly. "I didn't trap him. This wasn't planned, but we're dealing with it together."

He laughs, a cold, bitter sound. "Together? You think this is some fairytale?"

I straighten my spine, trying to muster some courage, but my voice is barely a whisper. "We care about each other. We're going to make this work."

Mr. Cross takes a step closer, his eyes narrowing. "Let me paint you a picture, Jennifer. Saint is meant for great things. He's meant to take over my company, to lead a multi-billion-dollar empire. He's meant to marry someone from a respectable family, someone who can help him, not drag him down."

His words sting, each one hitting like a dart. I can feel the weight of his disapproval, the sheer disgust in his voice.

"And what about you?" he continues, his voice a low growl. "You're just a nobody. A girl from the wrong side of town with no connections, no wealth, no future. You think you can provide for his child? You think you can give that child the life it deserves?"

I swallow hard, tears pricking at the corners of my eyes. I

cling to my belly, feeling the tiny life inside me, the life that Saint and I created together.

"He'll lose everything because of you," Mr. Cross says, his voice filled with venom. "His future, his inheritance, his place in society. You'll drag him down to your level, and he'll resent you for it. He'll resent the child. And you'll both be miserable."

His words paint vivid images in my mind—images of Saint's resentment, of a life filled with regret and misery. I can see the future he's describing, and it terrifies me.

"But there's a way out," he says, his voice softening slightly. "I'll make you a deal, Jennifer. Leave Saint. Cut him loose. Let him have the future he deserves. And I'll make sure you're taken care of. I'll give you enough money to raise the child. You won't have to worry about anything."

"You won't have to worry about a thing," Mr. Cross continues, his voice deceptively gentle. "The child will have everything it needs. The best schools, the best healthcare, the best of everything. And you, you can live comfortably. You won't have to struggle. You won't have to drag Saint down with you."

His words are like poison, seeping into my mind, planting seeds of doubt and fear. I can see the future he's painting—a future where Saint is successful, respected, and happy. And then I see the future he's warning me against—a future where Saint is miserable, resentful, and trapped.

"You're not good for him, Jennifer," he says, his voice a low murmur. "You're not good enough. You'll ruin his life. Is that what you want? To see him suffer because of you?"

Tears stream down my cheeks, and I can't hold them back any longer. I feel like I'm drowning, like I'm being crushed under the weight of his words, under the weight of the truth he's forcing me to face.

"No," I whisper, my voice barely audible. "I don't want that. I never wanted that."

He nods, a satisfied smirk on his lips. "Then do the right thing, Jennifer. Leave him. Let him go. Give him the future he deserves."

I feel a sob building in my chest, a overwhelming sense of despair washing over me. I look down at my belly, at the life growing inside me, and I feel a pang of guilt. I'm not good enough. I'll ruin his life. I'll ruin our child's life.

"I'll... I'll think about it," I manage to say, my voice choked with tears.

Mr. Cross nods, a victorious gleam in his eyes. "Good. Think about it, Jennifer. Think about what's best for Saint. Think about what's best for your child."

He turns and walks away, leaving me standing there, tears streaming down my face, my heart shattered into a million pieces.

THE TOWNHOUSE IS quiet when I walk in, my heart already tight in my chest.

I didn't expect to find it like this.

I pause just inside the doorway, stunned. My breath catches in my throat.

The entire living room is bathed in soft, golden candlelight. Dozens of them—on the mantle, the windowsills, lining the floor. Petals of deep red and blush pink roses are scattered across the polished hardwood, leading a trail toward the center of the room.

The furniture has been pushed aside.

In the center, a round white rug. A velvet box. And Saint.

Standing there in a black button-down, sleeves rolled up, nervousness etched across his otherwise confident face.

I blink rapidly, heart stuttering. My hands go to my belly.

"Saint," I whisper.

He smiles. But it's the soft kind—the one he reserves for moments like this. For *me*.

"I wanted it to be perfect," he says, voice rough with emotion. "Not because of the baby. Not because we're supposed to. But because I love you, Jennifer."

I step forward slowly, feeling like I'm floating through someone else's dream.

He reaches into his pocket and pulls out the box.

Opens it.

Inside is a ring so beautiful it steals the air from my lungs.

A platinum band, delicate but strong, with a radiant-cut diamond flanked by two small sapphires on either side. Elegant. Timeless. A little bold—just like Saint.

"It's your birthstone," he murmurs, nodding toward the sapphires. "I wanted it to look like *you*. Classic and unforgettable."

Tears flood my eyes before I can stop them.

He goes down on one knee.

And the image breaks me.

Because I should be smiling. Laughing. Saying yes without a second thought.

But my heart cracks instead.

He holds out the ring. "Jennifer Garcia... will you marry me?"

I take a step back, the sob catching in my throat before I can choke it down.

"Saint..."

He stands immediately, the joy in his eyes fading as he takes in my expression.

Something's wrong.

He knows it.

"What is it?" he asks softly. "Why are you crying like that?"

I try to speak, but the words are jagged glass. "I... I can't."

His brows draw together. "Can't what?"

"I can't say yes."

His whole body tenses. "Why?"

I look away, wiping at my tears. "Because I'll ruin you. Your dad said it, and he's right. You have a future waiting for you. A legacy. A company. And I'll only drag you down—"

He exhales sharply, stepping forward. "Stop. Don't say that."

"It's true," I whisper, my hands cradling my belly. "I'm just some poor girl with nothing. And you're—"

"No."

His voice is firm now. Steel beneath velvet.

"No, Jennifer. Those words didn't come from you. They came from *him*. What did he say to you?"

I shake my head, trying to push it away. "It doesn't matter—"

"It matters to me."

I take a breath, the pain slicing through me. "He found me outside my apartment. Told me I'd destroy your future. That I wasn't good enough. That you'd resent me and our baby."

Saint's jaw clenches. Fury flashes across his face, fast and hot.

"My father was never happy," he spits. "He doesn't know what love is. His marriages were cold, strategic things. He can't stand seeing someone else get what he never had. That's why he wants to sabotage this."

He steps forward, takes my face in his hands. Gentle. Grounding.

"But I'm not him."

I blink up at him, the tears still falling.

"I don't want a loveless empire. I want you. I want *this*. You, me, our kid. That's my legacy."

He pulls back slightly, his thumb brushing over my cheek.

"I would've proposed even if you hadn't gotten pregnant. Maybe not now, maybe after graduation, but it was always going to be you."

My breath stutters.

"I love you, Jennifer. I want to marry you because you're strong and smart and mouthy and brilliant. And because when I think about the future, you're the only thing I see."

I stare at him, everything inside me unravelling.

"But I'm scared," I whisper. "What if things change? What if you regret it someday—"

He silences me with a kiss.

Deep. Anchoring.

Then he rests his forehead against mine.

"Then I'll remind you every day that you're the best thing that ever happened to me."

I let the truth settle. Let it wash away the poison of his father's words.

He's right.

David Cross doesn't get to decide what love looks like.

I do.

We do.

I look down at the ring. Then up at the man I never saw coming but now can't imagine living without.

I nod, the tears falling again—but this time they're happy.

"Yes," I whisper. "Yes, I'll marry you."

Saint slides the ring on my finger, then pulls me into his arms like he's never letting go.

And I believe him.

THE BEDROOM IS DIM, lit only by the warm orange glow of the bedside lamp.

Outside, the world is quiet. Rain taps softly against the windows.

Inside, everything feels still. Safe.

I lie curled on my side, facing Saint. His hand is draped protectively over the swell of my belly, fingers splayed like he's trying to touch the baby through skin and bone.

My left hand rests on the pillow beside me.

The diamond catches the lamplight.

I still can't stop staring at it.

"You're doing it again," Saint murmurs, his voice thick with sleep and something softer.

"Doing what?"

"Staring like you can't believe I actually proposed."

I smile, blinking slowly. "I can't."

He chuckles, pulling me closer until I'm tucked beneath his chin.

"Well, believe it. You're mine now, officially."

"I was already yours."

He shifts back just enough to look at me. "Now you've got a ring that proves it."

I glance down again at the platinum band, running my thumb over the sapphire. "It's so perfect."

"Just like you."

I roll my eyes. "You're so corny."

He smirks. "Get used to it. Husband privilege."

My breath catches slightly at the word. *Husband.*

It's real now.

The proposal. The baby. The future.

His fingers trace lazy circles over my stomach. "They kicked today."

"I know," I whisper. "They're starting to move more. Especially when you talk."

He grins, eyes gleaming. "I've got a dominant voice."

"You've got a soothing voice," I murmur. "They know it."

Saint goes quiet for a minute, like he's trying to listen for the baby again.

Then: "Can I tell you something?"

"Always."

He swallows. "After you said no tonight... I thought I lost you. Just for a second. It felt like the ground disappeared under me."

I reach up and cradle his jaw, my thumb brushing the edge of his cheekbone. "I was scared."

"I know," he says. "But we've been scared before. And we're still here."

I nod, burying my face into his chest. "I love you so much, Saint."

His arms tighten around me.

"I love you more, Mrs. Almost Cross."

I laugh into his shirt. "We haven't even set a date yet."

"We'll figure it out."

"We have to graduate first."

He groans. "Don't remind me."

A pause. Then, softly: "Have you thought about names?"

My heart flutters. "A little."

He lifts an eyebrow. "Wanna try a few out?"

I giggle. "Okay. But if you say something like Blaze or Steel—"

"I was thinking...Alaric."

I burst out laughing. "You're not naming our child after a vampire."

"Fine. What about Luca? Or Sofia?"

I pause. "Sofia's beautiful."

"She'll have your eyes," he whispers.

I smile. "And his dad's temper."

He leans down and kisses me—slow and deep and reverent.

When we finally settle again, he keeps his hand over my belly, thumb brushing across my skin like a promise.

I fall asleep to the sound of his breathing.

His ring on my finger.

And his love wrapped around me like a second heartbeat.

TWENTY-TWO

Saint

WE DID IT.

Goddamn it, we did it.

Final grades are in, projects are done, professors are out of our lives, and as of this afternoon, we're officially free.

No more classrooms. No more assignments. No more pretending I give a shit about group work.

Just me, Jennifer... and the baby we're about to meet in less than two months.

I watch her now, across from me at the little candlelit table, the curve of her belly round and proud beneath her navy-blue wrap dress.

Her hair's curled soft around her shoulders, and the diamond on her finger sparkles every time she lifts her water glass. The ring still catches her off guard — she keeps touching it like she can't believe it's real.

I get it.

Some days I still look at her and wonder how the hell I managed this.

Jennifer Garcia. Mine. Carrying my son. Wearing my ring.

And finally, finally, I get to show her off the way I've always wanted to.

No more hiding in library corners. No more ducking past gossiping classmates. No more pretending she's just another girl.

She's not.

She's the girl.

My girl.

The waitress brings out our desserts—something chocolate and molten and probably too sweet—and gives Jennifer a little smile when she sets it down.

Then she glances at her hand. At the ring.

Her eyes dart to me. Then back to her.

"Oh," she says softly, smiling wider now. "Congratulations."

Jennifer blushes, but I grin.

"Thank you," I say, draping my arm over the back of Jennifer's chair. "We just got engaged."

"And we just finished college," Jennifer adds, pride blooming in her voice. "Graduation's in a week."

The waitress beams. "Wow. You guys are on a roll."

We are.

And I'm not even trying to be humble about it.

We killed this semester. I managed to graduate early just to stay by her side. She powered through finals while growing a whole human. And we did it together.

Now all that's left is... everything else.

When the waitress walks away, Jennifer leans into me a little, her hand settling on her belly like it always does.

I cover it with mine.

"Do you think he knows his parents are badasses?" I murmur.

Jennifer snorts. "I think he knows his dad is cocky."

"And his mom is brilliant."

"And hormonal."

I kiss her cheek. "Hot, brilliant, and hormonal. You're the full package, Garcia."

She rolls her eyes, but I see the little smile she's trying to hide.

"What if he comes early?" she asks suddenly, fingers brushing over the swell of her belly.

I look down, letting my hand spread across her bump. I can feel him kick, strong and confident, like he's already trying to get out and cause trouble.

"I'll be ready."

"You say that like you've read the parenting books."

"I skimmed the headlines."

She snorts again.

"We're calling him Mateo, right?" I ask, even though we've talked about it for weeks.

"Yeah." Her voice softens. "Mateo Saint Cross."

A thrill goes through me. Hearing it said out loud makes everything feel even more real.

"I like that," I say. "Strong name. He's gonna need it."

She looks up at me, her eyes soft. "You think your dad will ever—"

"No." I cut her off gently, but firmly. "He made his choice. And I've made mine."

I lower my voice, brushing my thumb across her hand. "You, me, and Mateo. That's it. That's the legacy I want."

She swallows hard, and I know she's holding back emotion. We've come so far from the beginning, from the hate and tension and fear and secrets.

I lean in close.

"You made me better," I whisper. "And now... now I get to spend the rest of my life proving I deserve this. You. Him."

She presses her lips to mine in the middle of the restaurant like she doesn't care who's watching.

And for once, we don't have to.

EPILOGUE

Jennifer

FOUR YEARS LATER...

THE MORNING SUNLIGHT spills through the kitchen windows, painting everything gold.

There's music playing softly—some acoustic indie song Saint loves, though he'll never admit it out loud. The scent of fresh bread wafts from the oven, and the faint clatter of alphabet blocks echoes from the living room.

I shift slightly in the doorway, resting one hand on my lower back and the other on the swell of my belly. Seven months pregnant, and I swear this baby's heavier than Mateo ever was.

Speak of the devil.

Tiny feet slap against hardwood, and a second later, our

three-year-old comes flying around the corner in his dinosaur pajamas, face smeared with something suspiciously chocolate.

"Mommy!" he yells, launching at me like a missile.

I catch him as best I can, laughing as I brace myself and squat awkwardly to his height.

"Easy, baby," I breathe. "Mama's carrying your baby sister, remember?"

He leans forward and plants a sticky kiss on my stomach. "Hi, baby!"

And just like that, I melt.

I stroke his wild black curls, already so much like Saint's. His nose crinkles with mischief, eyes gleaming.

"You've been into the brownies, haven't you?"

He shrugs.

I narrow my eyes. "Did Daddy say you could?"

Mateo doesn't answer.

Because at that moment, Saint steps into the room with a juice box in one hand and a towel slung over his shoulder. His shirt's rumpled. His sweatpants are riding low on his hips. His hair is sleep-mussed.

And he still looks like a walking sin.

"Don't look at me," he says, smirking. "He overpowered me."

"You're six foot two," I deadpan. "He's three."

"He's fast. And manipulative. I don't stand a chance."

Mateo runs back to the living room giggling, and Saint walks over, hands on my hips, eyes falling to my belly.

"She's been kicking a lot," I murmur.

"She knows I'm here." He drops to one knee and presses his lips to the top of my bump. "Hey, sweetheart. You letting Mommy sleep, or are you still practicing kickboxing at 3 A.M.?"

I thread my fingers through his hair, overwhelmed by the

sheer simplicity of this moment. Of him. Of us.

Years ago, I didn't think we'd survive.

Now we're thriving.

Saint walked away from his father's empire without looking back. We started small—a business of our own. Something sustainable. Something ours. I helped him build it brick by brick, and he trusted me every step of the way.

We haven't touched his trust fund. Not once. We haven't needed to.

Turns out, love and ambition are a lethal combination.

We're not just surviving. We're succeeding.

Together.

Saint rises to his feet and pulls me gently into his arms, careful of the baby bump between us.

"You're glowing," he murmurs, pressing a kiss to my jaw.

"I'm swollen. My ankles are pillows. I look like a whale. I've gained so much weight."

"You're a sexy pregnant mama," he insists. "And I like you like that."

I roll my eyes. "You're disgusting."

"You married disgusting."

I smile into his chest. "I did."

———

LATER, I lie curled on our bed, propped up with pillows. Mateo's napping in the next room. The house is still, quiet. Saint sits beside me, one hand absently stroking my thigh, the other resting on my belly.

He's shirtless, lazy and warm, a book about toddlers lying forgotten on his lap.

"Did you ever think we'd get here?" I ask quietly.

He looks over at me, eyes serious.

"I always hoped."

"I didn't," I admit. "I thought I'd mess it up. That I'd ruin you."

"You didn't ruin me," he says. "You *built* me."

I blink back tears.

"You saved me, Saint."

"We saved each other."

His palm moves slowly over my belly, his lips brushing my skin like a prayer.

"She's gonna have your mouth," he murmurs. "Sharp as hell."

"She'll have your eyes."

"God help me."

I laugh, eyes closing.

"I love you," I whisper.

"I love you more."

A beat of silence passes. And then—

"You gonna let me bully you in bed tonight?" he says, voice husky against my ear.

I snort. "If I can roll over."

"I'll help you. Gently. Like a sexy forklift."

"Saint!"

He grins, wicked and boyish and everything that still makes my heart race.

"Just sayin', you're irresistible when you're round and full of my baby. Hormonal and needy and—"

"Saint."

"Yes, wife?"

"I love you."

He softens instantly.

Leans in.

Kisses me like I'm still the center of his universe.

Like nothing—not time, not struggle, not fear—could ever touch us again.

And I believe him.

Because he's never let me fall.

And now, I know he never will.

ALSO BY KRYSTAL CLARK

Want to know what's next? Subscribe to my newsletter to be informed of new book releases and read exclusive excerpts. I release at least one book a month. You can be the first to know about sales, free ebooks, and special offers.

I have written more than 70 books with plenty of age gap, daddy kink, breeding, lactation, dark romance, mafia romance, hucow, and BDSM stories. Check out some of my other works!

If you like stories like this, start reading this steamy series with the first book: Knocked Up by My Ex's Dad.

Dark, sensual, spicy romances with an intense, consuming love story: Dominant Daddy's Captive Bride.

If you're interested in a steamy rom-com novella about a cold boss and his feisty employee, check out Sexting My Boss. This book has multiple steamy scenes but no kinks.

Love dark romances with milking/lactation kink? Check out Stalker Daddy's Milk.

If you're eager for short cowboy romance novellas with breeding, and other kinks, start my cowboy romance series with: Baby-making

If you like a full-length novel with plot, romance, and daddy-little girl dynamics, along with endless breeding and milking smut, check out: Knocked Up by My Ex's Dad

Like omegaverse erotica? Check out: Knot My Fated Mate

Alien's Omega Captive (MM)

Buy my box set collections, which contain 15 of my other books focused on breeding, daddy kink, and lactation.

Milky with Big Bellies

Taboo Daddy Short Stories Collection

Taboo Pregnant and Milked

And my other short stories:

Pregnant for My Alien Ex

Degraded by My Best Friend's Dad

If steamy monster romances with breeding kink, lactation, and pregnancy float your boat, try:

Maid for the Gargoyle Lord.

My Best Friend's Monster Dad

Kraken King's Bride

Arranged Marriage with a Werewolf

A Nanny for the Lich

Demon's Secret Baby

Milked by the Dragon

ABOUT THE AUTHOR

Krystal Clark is the author of over 70 spicy romance stories. Her books cater to specific kinks and often feature protective men with a 'daddy' vibe, breeding kink, pregnancy, and lactation/hucow/milking kink. So whether you're looking for a monster romance with pregnancy or a contemporary billionaire romance with a hucow, she has you covered.

Printed in Dunstable, United Kingdom